LIVING

GROWING UP

BEYOND

MEXICAN

BORDERS

IN AMERICA

• DAVID BOWLES • DOMINIC CARRILLO • ANGELA CERVANTES • ALEX TEMBLADOR •

e.E. CHARLTON-TRUJILLO • RUBÉN DEGOLLADO • CAROLYN DEE FLORES • XAVIER GARZA • AIDA SALAZAR • TRINIDAD GONZALES

SYLVIA SÁNCHEZ GARZA • ANNA MERIANO • DANIEL GARCÍA ORDAZ • DIANA LÓPEZ • JUSTINE MARIE NARRO • RENÉ SALDAÑA JR.

LIVING

GROWING UP

BEYOND

MEXICAN

BORDERS

IN AMERICA

EDITED BY *Margarita Longoria*

• GUADALUPE RUIZ-FLORES • GUADALUPE GARCÍA MCCALL • FRANCISCO X. STORK •

PHILOMEL BOOKS

PHILOMEL BOOKS

An imprint of Penguin Random House LLC, New York

First published in the United States of America by Philomel, an imprint of Penguin Random House LLC, 2021

Library of Congress Cataloging-in-Publication Data

Names: Longoria, Margarita, editor.
Title: Living beyond borders : growing up Mexican in America / edited by
  Margarita Longoria.
Description: New York : Philomel Books, an imprint of Penguin Random House LLC,
  2021. | Audience: Ages 12 up. | Audience: Grades 7–9. | Summary: "An
  anthology of short stories, essays, poetry, and comics about the Mexican
  American experience"— Provided by publisher.
Identifiers: LCCN 2021015489 | ISBN 9780593204979 (hardcover) | ISBN
  9780593204993 (ebook)
Subjects: LCSH: Mexican Americans—Literary collections. | CYAC: Mexican
  Americans—Literary collections.
Classification: LCC PZ5.L7295 2021 | DDC 810.9/86872—dc23
LC record available at https://lccn.loc.gov/2021015489

Printed in the United States of America

10 9 8 7 6 5 4 3 2 1

SKY

Edited by Liza Kaplan.

Design by Monique Sterling.

Text set in Goudy Old Style.

For my father, Jose "Rosie" Longoria. My hero.
And for my Three Bears: Eliseo, Michael, and Mateo—
my boys, my everything.

CONTENTS

Dear Reader   *ix*

Ghetto Is Not an Adjective by Dominic Carrillo   *1*

Yoli Calderon and Principal Hayes by Angela Cervantes   *12*

Warning Bells by Anna Meriano   *21*

I Want to Go Home by Justine Marie Narro   *34*

How to Exist in a City of Ghosts by Carolyn Dee Flores   *38*

Filiberto's Final Visit by Francisco X. Stork   *46*

CoCo Chamoy y Chango by e.E. Charlton-Trujillo   *58*

Tell Me a Story/Dime un cuento by Xavier Garza   *72*

My Name Is Dolores by Guadalupe Ruiz-Flores   *74*

"There Are Mexicans in Texas?":
How Family Stories Shaped Me by Trinidad Gonzales   *80*

Morning People by Diana López   *91*

Ode to My Papi by Guadalupe García McCall   *114*

The Body by the Canal by David Bowles   *116*

Is Half Mexican-American Mexican Enough?
by Alex Temblador   *133*

Sunflower by Aida Salazar   *142*

La Migra by René Saldaña Jr.   *150*

La Princesa Mileidy Dominguez by Rubén Degollado   *152*

Ojo by Sylvia Sánchez Garza   *185*

La Llorona Isn't Real by Xavier Garza   *200*

This Rio Grande Valley by Daniel García Ordaz   *201*

Acknowledgments   *203*

About the Authors   *205*

Once social change begins, it cannot be reversed. You cannot uneducate the person who has learned to read. You cannot humiliate the person who feels pride. You cannot oppress the people who are not afraid anymore.

– César Chávez

Dear Reader,

The idea for this anthology arose when our heritage came under attack in the media. Witnessing the constant spread of negative information fill my newsfeed, I felt compelled to do *something*. To fight back against the damaging rhetoric and biased images that clashed with the culture I lived and loved. To hear Mexicans being blanketly implicated as violent and as rapists, as illegal and bad people, infuriated me. This portrayal, meant to dehumanize and demonize our ethnic group, felt like an attack on our humanity and not the depiction of the Mexican people I knew.

I wanted a collection of stories that represented what it means to me to be a Mexican American living in America today. In these stories I wanted hope, family, friendship, and empowerment to shine through and help heal this hate. I wanted to explore our horrific past—the borders we have crossed, the obstacles we have pushed through, both metaphorically and physically—and acknowledge the self-imposed confines we often struggle with as a result of the oppression that has plagued our culture and our people for decades.

Through this collection of stories, personal essays, poetry, comics, and more, I wanted to educate others and celebrate the beauty and uniqueness of the Mexican American culture. Because the Mexican American people I know are resilient. We will not live in fear of who we are, or be ashamed of where we come from, and we will continue to show the world that we are seeds. Plant us in any environment and we will thrive. We are proud of who we are, and we are humble in our work. We have dignity; we try to embody the best of humanity. From doctors and CEOs to custodians and fieldworkers to teachers and more, the tapestry of our people, our labor, and our contributions to this country is woven tightly into the infrastructure of this land we call home.

I am a Tejana. I grew up along the southernmost tip of Texas in a place that borders Mexico called the Rio Grande Valley. Despite the violent beginnings that settled this area, the Valley is a warm and inviting place. Growing up where I did, I have always felt lucky to be able to experience the best of both worlds. To live on the cusp of two cultures, to be able to embrace, appreciate, and grow in two countries was an adventure that has helped shape who I am today. Yet even now I am reminded of the common misperceptions of and the injustices faced by those who live with Spanish surnames—from the belief that you must be fluent in Spanish to the assumption that you are not American to the discrimination and bullying Mexican Americans face from native English speakers.

This is made worse by the fact that crossing back and forth is normal for most of us living along the border—regardless of what side you live on. Whether it is to shop at a store, visit a doctor, travel across to work, or eat at a restaurant, border towns on both sides depend on each other to survive and to flourish. We are a blend of each other. My hope in creating this collection is that you, dear reader, may see a side of life, inside our culture, that is not often portrayed in the media.

After all, it is this misconception of life along the Mexico border that has made such an impact on the way many people perceive what it means to be of Mexican descent. I can still remember the fear I felt as a little girl when my family would travel north in Texas, out of the Valley, and the US Border Patrol would ask, "Are you American citizens?" There was no reason for me to be scared. I was always with my dad, and we were all American citizens, born and raised, yet I always felt uneasy. I remember asking my dad, "Why do they ask us that? What if they do not believe me? What if they do not believe you?" He would always pacify me with "They are just doing their job. They are looking for bad guys, they are looking for illegal activity, they are not going to hurt you, just tell them the truth." But this never made sense to me. "Then why don't they just ask us if we are bad guys? Why do they ask if we are American? We are coming from home. We live in America. Why are they asking us to declare our citizenship when we have never left the country?"

This is life for those of us living on the border.

When I moved away from home, discrimination came in more subtle ways. I can still remember being stunned when I was told my English was great "for a Mexican." I remember feeling perplexed when I was praised for my "extensive" vocabulary. And I remember the time my boyfriend and I were stopped by a police officer while driving around an affluent Houston neighborhood late one night, looking at the big pretty houses in a new truck my mother had just bought me. The officer wanted to know who owned the truck and what we were doing in that area. Over time, these kinds of incidents and statements began to anger me.

As Mexican Americans, we have always needed to defend who we are, where we were born, and prove to others that we are in fact Americans. Although I am proud to be an American, my Mexican heritage is one that I have always loved and fully embraced as well. Yet we are forced to be on the fence, not because we do not want to belong to both worlds, but because society demands that we choose a side. Where do we want to belong?

As Mexican Americans, we have always had battles to fight, stereotypes to break, prejudices to disprove, and stigmas to overcome. And as a collective people, we long to defend ourselves from the unjust. Our ancestors have pushed through many borders for us already, yet our work is still not done. The Mexican culture is full of life, full of color, and full of beauty. We are not a one-size-fits-all people; we come in all shapes, sizes, and hues. My parents raised me to see diversity as a gift, and I believe it is our differences that make each of us important.

This is the culture I wish to share with you. And I'm so grateful that many other Mexican Americans feel the same way.

Some of the best writers of Mexican American literature today have risen to the occasion in contributing to this anthology for you, our youth, our future. You are the best of all of us; you are our heart and soul. You will take the strides that have been paved before you and blaze your own trails, bigger and better. Wild hearts and passionate spirits live through you. You will make the difference; you will help to heal our plight; you will represent the real America.

Si vas a soñar, sueña en grande,

Margie

GHETTO IS NOT AN ADJECTIVE
by **DOMINIC CARRILLO**

Cell phone dead.

Not good for Senior Ditch Day—especially when you've got places to be.

I had no clue what time it was as I walked toward the closest bus stop on Thirtieth Street.

Ask the bus driver, I guess. This bus thing is still new to me.

Of all days for my car to not start . . . Correction: my parents' car. It was usually that, or rides with friends. Never the bus.

If I had just asked the bus driver earlier that day, then two stupid detours could've been avoided. Thankfully, the bus arrived at almost the same time I made it to the empty bus stop bench, where I noticed the cheesy ad of a slick, dark-haired real estate agent.

Trust Me: Mark Rodriguez, it read.

Must be a pocho like me. Half Mexican, half white. Not fully accepted in one world or the other. Too Mexican for some, not

Mexican enough for others. *I bet he can't even speak Spanish—kind of like me.* But did language have anything to do with it? Who made the rules on what being Mexican was or wasn't? I'd always been told to check a box—to fit in one category or the other. But it wasn't ever that easy. And why did it matter?

I stepped on the bus and flashed my all-day pass as if I were a public transit veteran. At the risk of blowing my cover, I asked the chubby driver if I was on the right bus—the one that continued through South Park, Golden Hill, and headed into downtown. He confirmed this with surprisingly little annoyance in his voice. I thought about asking him more questions. I had already messed up twice and been lost too much that day. So I lingered by the driver.

"What time is it?" I asked him.

The exhausted sighs of the few people waiting to get on behind me told me that one more question was one too many. But I stood there anyway.

The driver's thick head didn't move. His sunglass-covered eyes were laser focused straight ahead. I thought he didn't hear me at first.

Then he finally spoke. "Three twenty-six," he said. "Look, my *job* is to drive. Next question's gonna cost you a dollar."

Jesus Christ, where did the time go!? Sure, a broken-down car and some rookie bus mistakes would make me late to the Senior Ditch party downtown, but three hours? I could hear the Mexican late jokes already—the laughter of certain white boys who seemed to be experimenting with racism and what they could get away with.

I picked a seat toward the rear, closer to the Mexican junior high students in the back than those sitting near the front. Sitting in the back seemed more interesting because the students were actually talking to one another, lounging along the rear wall and on the side benches, making it a communal area—everyone facing inward. I didn't fit in, but I wasn't trying to either. I was just there to eavesdrop on my way downtown.

The most vocal were two teenage Latina girls with tightly pulled-back black hair and heavy eyeliner. They were sitting adjacent to me, chatting away, occasionally going into a whiny, singsongy Spanglish that was harsh on the ears. A Mexican guy with dark-rimmed glasses sat across from them. He looked more like a young college student who had recently adopted Che Guevara as his personal hero—or at least his fashion consultant. We both sat there, listening to the girls' chatter without staring directly at them, and knowingly glanced at each other once—aware that we were distracted by the same thing.

As the bus started toward downtown, the two teenyboppers' piercing voices, foul language, and shrieking laughter were becoming intolerable. They were in that junior high stage when obnoxiousness and vulgarity made someone more popular among their insecure peers. But I guess it was pretty normal teenage banter. Then they said it—a word I had previously given little to no consideration.

"That's so ghetto!" the skinnier one said.

"*You're* ghetto," the other snapped back.

The Che Guevara guy's eyes lit up and filled with fire. Now he turned toward them, his brow lowered in distress.

I didn't get it at first, but he'd obviously reacted to the word *ghetto*. I'd heard *ghetto* used in such a way before but thought nothing of it aside from its technical misuse.

"I am *not* ghetto," the skinny one replied sassily.

"You are toooo GHETTO!" the other repeated.

"What?" Che interrupted them.

He seemed agitated, but more out of intense philosophical interest than raw aggression—as if he were an impassioned professor of social justice. Maybe it was the thick-rimmed eyeglasses. Whatever it was, the girls stopped their bickering. Shocked into silence, they turned their powdered noses and blackened eyebrows up at him.

"*What* does that mean?" he repeated.

"*What* are you talkin' about?" the skinny one said with attitude. Her friend snorted, clearly pleased with the rude comeback.

They weren't ready for an interruption or disapproval from some stranger on the bus. They were unaware of the gravity of the situation.

So was I.

"What does calling someone *ghetto* even mean?" Che asked.

The two girls looked both surprised by the question and puzzled by what may have seemed like too obvious an answer—an answer to a question they'd probably never considered. The more talkative flaca with flashy fingernails and a black Sharpie in her hand spoke up.

"*Ghetto* means"—she hesitated—"bad—you know—dirty or poor or ugly-looking."

"Yeah, all those things," her friend chimed in.

Che nodded and smirked in both acknowledgment and dis-appointment, as though he'd expected that exact answer from them. Then he leaned over more deliberately, crouching toward them with his elbow on his knees. He pushed his glasses higher up on his nose. It looked as if he were preparing to spring on them, like a lion ready to pounce.

"*Ghetto* is not an adjective." He said it in a calm yet com-manding voice.

The two girls turned to each other in what seemed to be con-fusion and discomfort. *Awkward.* By the looks on their faces, they probably didn't even know what an adjective was.

Che repeated, with growing intensity and clear enunciation, "*Ghetto* is not an adjective. It is a noun. It's the place where I live."

All of a sudden, that the bus was moving south, that there were over twenty other people on it, and that it was the middle of a comfortable San Diego afternoon didn't matter. This large vehicle had become a vessel—a stage—for a poetic, mysterious man to express to two captive girls (and all of us other pas-sengers) his perspective on what *ghetto* meant to him. They had no idea that their use of the word might disturb someone so deeply. And neither did I. But it must have meant the world to Che, because he rose to the occasion. Literally.

He stood up and continued what appeared to be part soapbox rant and part spoken-word poetry:

"For me it's Barrio Logan to be exact, but that lone fact is insignificant."

He made the words *exact* and *fact* punch us in the face with emphasis, rhythm, and a cadence that sounded well practiced. Yeah, this guy was a pro. He continued, to the girls' surprise, with a driving sense of purpose:

> "There's no Sherman, or Logan, or Shelltown to those on the
> outside looking in.
> It's all ghetto to them.
> Safely kept at a distance—
> mostly imagined on pixelated screens
> or glanced through car windows at high speeds.
> And it's okay, as long as we stay in it,
> except in transit
> between working kitchens
> and keeping things clean..."

Che paused then and took a big breath for the first time. He glanced at me, noticed that I was paying attention, then glared back at the now more attentive girls—all of us in awe of what one word had sparked in this guy.

> "Ghetto is not an adjective because it's a place
> that does not fit one description
> like crime-ridden, gang-infested, dirty manifestation
> no doubt a result of our news and screens
> bombarding us with well-edited crime scenes.
> Yes, I've seen a young teen
> with a shiny silver gun in his hand

and tats in between
sirens and gunshots,
yelling and screams
boxed in by conveniently constructed freeways
that still segregate
pollution and stress
causing our health to disintegrate.
Immobilized by poor public education,
disconnected teachers waiting for vacations
—and their credentials
leaving untapped potential to linger in subservience.
Like servants, we're kicked around all day,
picking, cooking, and cleaning—praying for change.
But how will this change?
When words like ghetto *are washed into our brains*
every day, by TVs, movies, video games,
and you!
When I hear you utter the word ghetto *in disdain,*
it pains me to associate my house and my name.
It's this invisible virus that infects us the most
through a simplistic, linguistic bacterial host,
a flippant adjective for some—a reality for most.
Madness has turned the word ghetto *into an adjective.*
Unfortunately, for now, it's where I live."

Che took another deep breath. Absorbed the scene. He had all eyes locked on him. He had to have practiced this poem at least a hundred times. The delivery was polished and near perfect. Everyone on the bus listened, either waiting for the next line or for some authority figure to intervene and pull the plug on this revolutionary poet. I was impressed by Che's courage, presence, and passion—but he wasn't finished. Sensing his audience's interest had grown, Che amplified his volume when he resumed:

"However,
I see ghettos that don't fit your ugly descriptions . . .
I see families at dinner in joint celebrations.
I see kids playing soccer, and scores of elation.
I see the faces of the elderly in exaggeration.
I see friends greeting and laughing at the bus stop.
Even a rare scene with a considerate cop.
I see houses painted vibrant colors
that suburban HOAs would ban.
I hear loud music, passion, and see all-natural tans.
I feel the pulse of the moment and the beating of drums.
Beautiful murals, loving people, and harmless bums.
So, if not the mainstream media, and not the TV,
at least let's start it—just you and me.
And not ghettoize our lives,
our roots and our ways.
Know the meaning of our words
and question and say:
'Yes, I live in one of many ghettos'
—often separated, misrepresented, or ignored.
I'm in a favela. I'm in a slum.

But I don't need no more slumlords!

So don't trap us with your words

that berate the place I live.

And remember, please remember:

GHETTO

is NOT an adjective. . . ."

Everyone was silent as the bus jerked to its next stop. I had never seen such an impromptu public performance, and I doubt anyone else on that bus had either. We all should have applauded in unison. We should've given him an award, but we didn't. It all happened too fast.

Seconds after he finished, Che hastily grabbed his messenger bag as the bus doors opened. For some unknown reason, he glanced at me and tossed a folded paper on my lap. It was his poem. *The* poem. Could he tell that I was part Mexican? Did he sense that I was trying—for the first time—to figure out what that even meant? Before I could look up and say thanks, he was gone. He walked down the bus aisle, a few people quietly praising him as he passed by their seats, but he exited without another word, adding even more dramatic effect to the whole scene.

I looked out the window and watched him walk triumphantly southbound down the hill toward Barrio Logan—the "ghetto" he had referred to. I had never been there—never thought of going there, actually. It was south of the 94 freeway, and I hadn't even driven through out of habit, but also lack of necessity, I guess. It made me question my own Mexican-ness, though.

Barrio Logan was the "most Mexican" neighborhood in San Diego, yet I'd never set foot in it. And Che was right. I had no idea what it was like in there, or any other so-called ghetto—only what others had made me believe over the years. His recitation was unbelievable, and his last line echoed in my head:

Ghetto *is NOT an adjective!*

The bus pushed forward. I looked back at the two teenage girls. They were both scrunching their faces in bewilderment and disapproval—almost disgust. They whispered a few inaudible words back and forth until the flaca blurted out:

"¡Que loco!"

Had they listened to a word? It seemed that the intended audience for Che's epic poem had already dismissed him as crazy. They didn't get it at all—a shame. Then they resumed their gossiping at low volume.

On to the next thing, I thought. Online chatting, gossip, and extra emojis. TikToks. Highlights. Fails. Football or some other sport. Flipping through endless photo feeds. The next best Netflix show. All distractions, just like Che had said.

I turned to look at the rest of the passengers. Heads down, staring at phones or gazing straight ahead. It was as if this epically performed poem was forgotten less than thirty seconds after it had happened. Had anyone really listened?

Then it hit me: the paper in my hand. The poem he'd given to me. *Why me?* Could it mean that Che wanted me to be the messenger? Could I share this with the world somehow? Or was it meant especially for me? And if I accepted this mission, what would happen? Seriously, holding that poem, I felt like Neo in the Matrix, having to choose between the blue and the red pill.

A choice.

If I accepted Che's mission—to share, to question, to rethink, to seek the truth for myself—it might make me more Mexican. Or maybe it would just make me more true to myself, a combination of sides and flavors to all be embraced.

As the bus cruised down the hill toward downtown, I wondered for the first time that day if that was where I really wanted to go—to a rich, private-school-kid party in a penthouse overlooking San Diego Bay? *On to the next thing.* For some odd reason, the answer was simple: *No.* I never felt like I belonged at those parties anyway.

It hit me then that all those detours—all the difficulty of the day—had happened for a reason. And now I sat with Che's poem in my hand. *A sign.* I was convinced.

I'd be choosing my detour this time. Finding my own way.

So I leaned toward the emergency stop cord that ran along the length of the bus.

And I pulled.

YOLI CALDERON AND PRINCIPAL HAYES

by ANGELA CERVANTES

If **you want** to know the truth, and I suppose you do, I've never even been to Mexico, Mr. Hayes. You're surprised, right? Have you been to Mexico?

Wait, how many times? Wow. Five times is a lot. Let me guess . . . Cancún, right? *Ding! Ding!* Winner! Is that photo behind your desk your family and you in Cancún?

It looks like paradise. Isn't it loco, Mr. Hayes? You and your kids have been to Mexico five times and yet the Mexican American girl sitting in your office has never been to Mexico. Wild, right?

My parents are the ones from Mexico. Like, from real Mexico. Not the touristy Mexico that you visited. Not the part where everyone speaks to you in English, accepts American dollars, and serves you two-for-one sugary-sweet margaritas with cheap tequila. That's Cancún. That's not Mexico.

Don't get me wrong, I wouldn't turn down a trip to Cancún.

Maybe someday I'll go, you know. It'd be cool to know Mexico beyond what I see on the news and what my parents tell me about it. When I go, I'll visit the *real* Mexico and see family. They live in the part of Mexico where no one speaks English, where you have to pay with pesos and they drink jamaica. And they sip tequila. They don't shoot it like college kids on spring break. There are some really good tequilas that are made to be sipped. I tried some at my primo's baptism last summer. Smooth. Yet most people think there's only the cheap spring-break tequila. It's also how lots of people think of Mexicans. They think there is just one type of us. Did you try tequila in Cancún?

You don't drink? Then why did you go to Cancún?

For the beach? It was a family trip. I get that. Do you speak Spanish when you're in Cancún?

You don't? Not even an easy *hola* or *más guacamole, por favor*?

You should try. I can give you a few words to practice for the next time you go. I speak Spanish, but it's not perfect. My mom says I speak Spanish often enough to get me into trouble, but not enough to get me out. Isn't that funny? And here I am in trouble, and I'm not sure speaking Spanish *or* English will save me. I did what I did. And I know this talk won't change anything, but you should know my side of the story. I don't just go around smacking people for no reason.

My side of the story doesn't start today in the hallway. It starts with my family. My parents brought me here when I was just a little seed in my mom's womb. Even though my parents chose to come here, they mostly speak Spanish and they hang on to our Mexican heritage.

At my home, it's Spanish only. And there is never any McDonald's on our dining table. Only corn tortillas warmed on the comal and snuggled up in towels. I could talk about the other foods, like caldo de camarones, enchiladas, plates of carne asada and nopales, but it'd only make us both hungry.

Do you like Mexican food?

Burritos? I knew you were going to say that. How? I just knew. Okay, I knew it because that's what all the non-Latinx people say. It's always burritos and tacos. As if that's all the Mexican food in the world. I'm not offended. It just is what it is.

I bet your favorite Mexican restaurant in town is . . . Cactus Grill? Border Burritos? Señor Jalapeño? Los Sombreros—

Got it. I mean, Señor Jalapeño is fine if you're really dying for a smothered burrito, but that's not Mexican food. And all the serapes they hang on the wall and all the free baskets of chips with mild salsa they serve you cannot even begin to replace what my mom and dad can cook on the stove.

What I'm trying to say is that there is no McDonald's and no Netflix at my house. It's all Spanish TV. If I want to watch the Kardashians or Netflix, I have to go over to my friend Pilar's house.

Yes, Pilar Cordero, our sophomore class president. We're best friends, but so far, her overachieving hasn't rubbed off on me and—

What?

You're right. So far, my troublemaking hasn't rubbed off on her. Thank goddess, right? Yes, I know she's a saint. Everyone tells me that. I'll be sure to let her know you said nice things about her. She tries to be a good influence on me, but it didn't work today.

Anyway, what I was saying was that my dad likes to tell me over and over: We didn't come here to eat McDonald's and watch the Kardashians. We came for a better life.

You came, I always remind him. I had no choice in the matter. I was born a few months after my dad sent for my mom to join him here. I have never known Mexico like they have, but somehow I'm proud of being from there just as much as I am proud of being an American. I really am. I'm a Mexican American. I don't hyphenate it. I don't call myself Hispanic. Latina is okay. Latinx is a little better. By calling myself Mexican American, I choose to claim Mexico—not reject it. It was my parents' country. It's also mine. Same with the United States. It's mine too. I don't have to choose one or the other.

What? *I am* telling my side. I'm not trying to stall anything. This has *everything* to do with why I smacked that stupid girl. Just let me finish—

Wait a minute. You think *stupid* is too harsh? You're shaking your head at me because I called her stupid? Do you think it was harsh when she told me to go back to Mexico, Mr. Hayes?

You do. So, we agree on that point. She was being racist. So I smacked her. I wanted to smack her the same way those words hit me across the face. I smacked her for all of the other Mexican American students who've also been told to go back to Mexico. And did you hear that her friends laughed when she said that to me? Laughed.

Talk about harsh.

I know it was against school rules to hit her. You're the principal. I get that you know the rules better than anyone. I know violence is never right, but what about the violence of words? Is there a school rule against that? Is she going to be suspended too?

Yeah, right. She's the victim.

Her busted lip will be fine. It'll heal. But maybe my action is the thing that will keep her and her friends from ever saying something like that to another Mexican American student again. I did what your school rules couldn't, and yet *I'm* the one being punished. *I'm* the one called to your office.

Are all those posters just a big lie? You know, the posters you have all over the hallways. If you didn't believe words were powerful, why would you have them freakin' plastered all over the school? Maybe if Laura had read that poster, the one posted up outside the gym that says, *Treat others as you wish to be treated*, none of this shit would have happened.

Sorry, I didn't mean to curse. Are you going to suspend me for that, too?

Okay, so you obviously think I shouldn't have smacked her. Was I just supposed to walk away? What if it was you, Mr. Hayes? What if you were told to go back to . . . ? I don't know, Norway? Scotland? England? The suburbs?

I swear I'm not making excuses. I'm just trying to share how I feel. In all of this, no one has even asked me how I feel. Everyone ran to Laura. Everyone comforted Laura. Are you all right, Laura? Do you need anything, Laura?

Fine. Go ahead and have your secretary call my parents if you think we're getting nowhere. Where were you hoping to go?

The thing is, no one can pick me up right now. My parents work. They're always working. They came here for a better life, and for them a better life means working to make money and sending me to school so I can get an education. My dad works at the dog food cannery until eight p.m. His boss never lets him off early. Not even one time when I fell at school and needed stitches. Pilar's mom came and got me. Yes, Mrs. Cordero. She's a saint just like her daughter. We agree on that point.

My mom can't come during the day either. She has a very demanding job. She's a seamstress for one of the fanciest shops here in town. You probably know it. She makes alterations on wedding gowns. Mostly she has to take out the dresses because the nervous brides are eating too much, but they scream and accuse my mom of getting the measurements wrong and making the dresses too tight. My mom says all she can do is smile and nod. She knows it's their fault. They are eating too many smoth-ered burritos and free baskets of chips at Señor Jalapeño. At least the chubby brides keep my mom's sewing machine hum-ming. It's the last thing I hear before I fall asleep and the first thing I hear when I wake up. She'll be home a little after six. So if you were hoping to sit them down in this nice office during work hours to talk about me—their troubled daughter—you'll be waiting a long time.

Also, like I said, their English isn't good. So if you want to talk to my parents, you better call the school translator,

Mrs. Ochoa, to help. Or I could translate . . . but I'm not sure you'd want me to. Probably not, right? Things might get a little twisted if I tell it.

Mrs. Ochoa already knows where I live. She's been to my house twice this school year. Once she came when there was a soccer game on. Bad timing. In my casa, it's all fútbol. No basketball, no American football, just Chivas and Americas and, of course, my dad's favorite team: Monarcas from the state of Michoacán. When fútbol is on, nothing else exists. Mrs. Ochoa ended up staying to watch the whole game with us. They're compadres now, which means friends who have become family.

Monarcas? You've never heard of them? Not surprised. They're a Mexican team. It means "monarchs"—kings and queens, right, but it's also the name for those famous butter-flies. You've seen them, yeah? In Michoacán—where my family is from—there are parks full of monarch butterflies. Do you know about the monarca, Mr. Hayes?

Just a little? The monarch butterfly is amazing. It migrates from one end of North America to the other, never losing its path through the Canadian forest, through the Midwest back to Michoacán, Mexico. It always knows where it comes from and how to get back there, regardless of the miles between where it flies and how far it travels from home. Kind of like my mom and dad. They came all the way from Mexico to the Midwest, and then they had me in a little leaf.

Kidding!

I was born at Mercy Hospital. Fifteen years later, here I

am. And maybe I'm more of a gross, sticky baby caterpillar than a butterfly right now. Maybe I'm still transforming into a monarca. Maybe that's why that stupid girl pissed me off. She told me to go back to where I come from. That's like telling my parents that all their hard work and sacrifice doesn't matter. That's like telling me I don't belong here when I belong just as much as she does. I know I belong because my parents chose this path.

Hold up. I take things too personally? Is there a way to turn off your heart? Teach me then, Mr. Hayes. Tell me, did anyone tell that girl to turn off her heart? Did you? I didn't think so.

What? Yes, I know the monarch eats milkweed. My mom puts some out for the butterflies in our garden. Did you know that milkweed is poisonous to people, but not to the monarca? It's true. You can look it up.

Use it as fuel? Like, take the words Laura thought would hurt me and instead use them to fuel me and become the monarca? I see what you're saying, I do. But can I ask you something? I'm not trying to get all deep or argumentative, but why do Mexican American girls like me have to eat this poison at all? Is this the only way to become a glorious monarch? That seems unfair. Really messed up.

How much will I have to take in? What poison do white girls have to drink to become better people? Or are they just born to become butterflies? Must be nice.

Do you believe I'm a monarca, Mr. Hayes?

You do? Thanks. You're not so bad after all. Pilar always said that you're reasonable.

I think this talk has helped. I'm not going to forget where I come from and where I can go. I won't be the poison. I choose to be the monarca.

Just one more thing, Mr. Hayes. Do you really have to suspend me?

WARNING BELLS

by ANNA MERIANO

Five minutes after she finishes yelling, Mom comes back into the kitchen. "Well," she huffs, "what are you pouting about?"

I guess that's what breaks the numb feeling in my legs and sends me stumbling to my room, where I can curl up on the floor and finally cry. I'm so tired, but I can't sleep. My thoughts don't fit in my head, and my breaths don't fit in my chest. I don't know how long I lie there, clutching my hands together, before I give up and let them go.

It's just scratches, I tell myself, watching the faint white lines turn red on the pinkie side of my curled fist. It's not like I have to call any hotlines or anything. The pain is already dulling, and I dig the fingernail of my left thumb into the largest scratch until it throbs again. It's nothing, really.

I know better than to trust myself, though.

It was never a question of who I would live with. I've spent a few nights at my dad's new apartment, but it smells like dust and disinfectant and hallway cigarettes, and I can never sleep there. Besides, Dad is an extrovert. He comes from a huge family; he likes his hunting trips and summer adult soccer league and the army of tiny middle school jocks he coaches after school. He never knew what to do with his one quiet daughter except play with me when I was fun and hand me off to Mom when I wasn't.

Mom was yelling about my grades, but it isn't really about grades. It's about proving that I'm *her* daughter, that I'm doing everything *her* way, that I'm following *her* values. Like everything else, it's really about Dad.

My grades aren't even bad. I'm passing everything. Ms. Delgado just got pissy when I stopped turning in my essays. And I guess I used to be a try-hard, turning everything in a week early and a page longer than it was supposed to be, so now she's trying to "remotivate" me. You'd think an English teacher would know that's not a real word.

I'm so tired of Ms. Delgado thinking she's changing the lives of all the Latinas in her class just because she assigns Sandra Cisneros and Toni Morrison instead of Jane Austen—like we're not all skimming the SparkNotes either way. She talks about her "abuela the immigrant" to try to connect with us, but my grandparents are from Texas and California, and anyway, it's all just a scam to get us to write our essays.

I stopped writing essays because I was tired of the way she smiled at me when she handed them back, and the scribbled purple-pen comments saying that the world Needs My Voice in these trying political times. Because *that's* what's been missing from the world—a ninth grader from Houston telling people that using hate crimes as a basis for your government and ignoring the rising sea level is bad, actually.

I'm so tired of these trying political times, and I'm tired of trying to care about the newest protests and the hashtags and the kids who die or almost die and get fifteen minutes of fame from the adults who have all the money and the clout and the thoughts and prayers but don't actually do anything.

You would think Mom and Dad could have a least agreed on the idea of protests, since they're both decent humans and Latinos, and they care about the environment and don't like hate crimes—but they still couldn't. Mom said Dad's idealism was shooting itself in the foot, and Dad said Mom was a centrist coward.

Still, that didn't stop me from going to a protest a few years ago, where a mother cried into a microphone and begged for a world where war didn't come to classrooms. But it didn't fix anything.

"It's Texas," Mom said when the protests lost steam and the laws didn't change. "What did you expect?"

Dad said it was a terrible thing to say, but he couldn't really deny that she was right.

I wanted to believe in the protests, but they never fixed anything. I wanted to believe in my parents, but they only know how to make things break.

Neither of their voices ever changed the world for the better.

~~~

It's midnight.

In the kitchen, the cheap plastic radio crackles to life with the wailing notes of a country song. Dad bought that radio years ago—a bright purple alarm clock that doesn't even run on batteries—thinking he was prepping the house for an emergency. Mom looked at it with such contempt, but she didn't say anything. Now it haunts us by turning itself on, trying to wake the house up at midnight every night since last month's power outage, and Mom *still* doesn't say anything, and I don't know how to reset it, so it never gets fixed. Every night I'm the only one awake to hit the button that turns the alarm off until the next night when it happens again, and I'm so, so tired of it.

I shuffle to the kitchen, holding my hand in a fist so the scratches pull and strain. The country song buzzes with static and sickly sweet nostalgia, but when I turn it off, the kitchen falls still and silent and that's worse. I reach into my pocket for my phone, but I left it upstairs on the floor of my room. I sigh, turn to leave the creepy kitchen, and that's when something whispers my name.

Daniela.

The hair on my arms lifts, but my feet weigh heavy on the floor like they're made of carved stone. The clouds shift, sending a beam of moonlight shining through the window, and my ears are ringing like bells and my temples pound like I'm on an airplane and I feel like I might throw up. My knees buckle and I fall in slow motion and find my cheek pressed to the ground for the second time tonight.

When my body stops its sudden mutiny, I push myself up onto my elbows. The kitchen isn't empty anymore. A tall, wide figure blocks the window, silver moonlight outlining its edges and cutting sharp lines of shadow across its form.

I should stand, or run, or scream.

"Daniela."

The voice is calm and stern, and I get strong middle school assistant principal vibes. I sit up straighter while the figure steps toward me, catching the light of the purple radio clock face. She kind of *looks* like a middle school assistant principal, in spite of the metal bells hanging off her cheeks, the gauzy rainbow of woven cloth making up her dress, and the crown of feathers circling her head. Like a middle school assistant principal who runs one of the Aztec dance groups that perform downtown on Cinco de Mayo and el 16 de Septiembre. Mom and Dad used to love taking me to all the Mexican and Chicanx pride events, and I used to like it too until I got older and couldn't wrap my head around how it's possible to dance with such fierce colorful joy while shouldering a legacy of so much pain.

This mystery apparition doesn't look like she came here to dance, though. Something in her expression says, *I don't have a single ounce of patience left*, which is probably why she reminds me of someone who spends their days corralling preteen punks.

I'm either about to be murdered by the weirdest home invader ever, or I should have called one of those hotlines earlier because I am not okay.

"What?" I ask. Mom would scold me if I gave her that attitude. "What do you want? What are you?"

"'What'?" the figure asks, head swiveling as she inspects the kitchen. "Not 'who'?"

"The what is a more immediate concern." This stranger doesn't seem to belong in the realm of reality, and I don't know if I'm facing a ghost or a dream or a LARPer or a serious mental health issue, and until I figure that out, I can't do anything about it.

The figure nods. "I thought you might know me." She sounds disappointed, and that, at least, gives me something familiar to latch on to. Another adult disappointed that I didn't perform for them. I get to my feet even though I barely come up to the chest of my potential murderer.

"Sorry, I must've missed your viral video. Are you going to fill me in?"

She smiles and looks down her nose at me in a way that makes me feel a lot less clever than I did a second ago.

"But you do know me," she says. "You've seen my likeness before, and heard my story."

Why is this giant feather-wearing bell-jingling person acting like one of the old people at Dad's parties who always come up to me and tell me how much I've grown since the last time they saw me? I stare up at the hard planes of her face, unfamiliar and unimpressed. She sighs heavily and then looks down to meet my eyes.

I definitely don't know her, because I would remember eyes like hers. I've never met anyone who looked so frustrated, so tired—not even an assistant principal, not even the speaker at the protest I went to. For a second my fingers forget that I gave up drawing before I gave up writing essays, and they twitch to shape the depths of those eyes in a sketchbook.

The last time I carried a sketchbook around—the memory hits me violently, swallows me up in a wave of sensations—was the summer after sixth grade during the trip to Mexico City with Dad's family (Mom hated group vacations and mostly stayed in the hotel). My bangs were growing out, and my braces were orange. We were visiting museums when I wanted to get ice cream. My cool older prima Melody, who had been to the city a million times to visit the other side of her family, was enjoying playing tour guide for her more gringified relatives. She was telling me and our littlest prima Ellery a story—she told us so many stories that day, but right now I'm only reliving one, only feeling the tickle of hair on my cheek as I stare up at the huge stone disc that Melody says is a dismembered goddess—an attempted murderer who became the moon. Preteen me flips open her sketchbook and draws Coyolxauhqui, starting with her eyes.

The memory fades, and I drop the hand that was about to brush imaginary hair out of my face. The figure's face is turned up again, but her mouth has settled into a more satisfied line.

This can't be real, and I refuse to say it.

"Are you freaking Coyolxauhqui?" I blurt in spite of my best intentions.

She doesn't answer.

"That's impossible. That doesn't even make sense. You're . . . mythical. And dead."

In the story, Coyolxauhqui and her younger siblings wanted

to kill their suspiciously pregnant mom, but the joke was really on them when the baby was born fully grown and armed, and he hacked them to pieces. He was the god of war or something, and threw all his murderous siblings down the mountain, chunk by bloody chunk, and I guess the dismembered body parts caught enough bouncing or rolling momentum to pop straight up into the sky, and that's how we got the moon and the stars.

Which is all kind of metal, but extremely doesn't answer the question of whether or not I'm about to be murdered.

"'Dead' is imprecise at best," Coyolxauhqui says. "I am the enemy and opposite of my brother Huitzilopochtli, and how can he exist without his opposite? He watches what is harsh and bright in the world, and I watch what is dark."

She gives me a look when she says that, and I clap my left hand over the scratches on the right. Oh no. I know that careful, concerned look, the look that says, *I'm not mad, I just want you to talk to me.* Oh no.

"Are you here to Teach Me a Lesson? Did Ms. Delgado put you up to this?"

I know it's sort of a nonsense thing to ask the pre-Columbian goddess in your kitchen, but it's sort of nonsense to *have* a pre-Columbian goddess in your kitchen, and I'm getting the sneaking suspicion that this one is trying to "remotivate" me into caring about something. Anything.

"Whatever you think you're doing here, I would very much like to be excluded from this narrative. I don't need you."

"Of course." Coyolxauhqui frowns. "You don't need anyone.

You already exist as your own opposite, enough darkness to overwhelm your bright light."

I knew it. I knew she was gearing up to Help the Troubled Teen. "Just tell me what you want or leave me alone."

"You'd rather I speak plainly? I'm here because you are infuriating."

Okay. I wasn't expecting that. But it hardly seems fair; I haven't done anything to anyone.

"Me?"

Coyolxauhqui raises an eyebrow like, *Did I stutter, bitch?* and I suddenly remember that this moon lady was fully ready to murder her mom just because she got pregnant from some floating ball of feathers that wasn't her husband.

"I didn't do anything to you. Sounds like you have anger issues."

"Anger issues," Coyolxauhqui repeats with a super unsettling hint of a smile. "Yes, I definitely had anger issues. Who could blame me? I cared about honor. I felt the betrayal of my mother so deeply in my bones that I turned against my own family, my flesh . . . I wanted to kill her."

I drop my eyes to the floor even though I already know the story. I don't like the rage burning in Coyolxauhqui's eyes. I don't want to recognize it.

But the moon lady isn't giving me an easy out. "You feel betrayed," she says, "just like I did."

"Well, I never planned to murder anybody over it, so I guess I'm not violent like you. And your mom didn't *actually* cheat. Mine did." With a grad student at her college—not her department, so at least it wasn't quite as immoral as it could have been. A white philosophy PhD candidate with a wispy mustache who is proudly apolitical and aggressively inoffensive. That's the featherweight straw that broke my parents' marriage.

My nails dig into my palms. Coyolxauhqui moves quick, snatching my wrists and forcing my hands open with surprising strength for someone who must be a figment of my imagination.

"What do you call this, if not violence?"

I pull my hands away and stuff them into the front pocket of my hoodie. "I call it not plotting to murder an infant, so I'm still coming out ahead in this comparison."

The moon lady gives me that patronizing expression I hate, the face adults make when they think it's just too funny how wrong you are.

"You remember that fact so well, but there are many ways to read my story."

"Aren't there always?" Maybe Ms. Delgado did send this vision. She seems like the type who would dabble with crystals and velas and summoning annoying spirits of indigenous gods on the weekends.

"Scholars have seen it as a metaphor for the day overtaking the night, the wartime triumph of one people over another. It is a history, a metaphor, and a moral all in one."

"You really need to meet my English teacher. Also, convenient that turning it into a metaphor glosses over the whole murdering-a-baby thing and makes you seem like the victim."

"I was ripped limb from limb for my mistakes."

"Mistakes?" That word and her tone and her infuriating half smile make me see red. "A typo is a mistake! You deliberately plotted matricide!" She can't smile calmly and pretend there's no villain here. She can't just erase what she did.

"My mistakes . . ." Coyolxauhqui starts to speak, but I refuse to hear another cowardly confession.

"Let me guess, you had a reason! You had no choice! 'Oh, I'm not perfect, I'm doing my best!' " I echo Mom's words, the ones she threw out the only time we ever talked about why Dad left. "It's such bullshit. Maybe stop making mistakes if you can't handle the consequences. And don't expect me to say it's all okay!"

Coyolxauhqui doesn't look away the whole time I talk, even when I realize I'm shouting. She stays quiet for so long after I stop that I clench my fists and shut my eyes. My words feel like they're boomeranging back at me, like they always do when it gets quiet, telling me that *I'm* the one making mistakes that no one can forgive.

But under Coyolxauhqui's steady gaze, they also sound wrong.

"You hold on to your sharpness so tightly, little warrior. It's no wonder you cut yourself."

"I'm tired," I say, and I don't even know if I'm answering her or changing the subject. "Can you please talk like a normal person?"

Coyolxauhqui tilts her head to one side. "You are angry. You are hurt. You feel the pain of the world and the pain of your family and the pain of being alive."

I want to tell her to shut up, but my throat isn't working. She reaches for my wrists and pulls my hands close to her face, and my scratches burn when she looks at them.

"You know that healing is change and change means sacrifice. But this is wrong. This is not healing."

I try to pull my hands away, but I can't. The lines on the side of my hand and the crescent-shaped trenches in my palms are glowing silver and hot, and I see matching lines glowing across Coyolxauhqui's body, wounds that are both scarred and fresh, bleeding light and breaking her body apart.

"The people who think they own all the power and light of this world, you already know what they are capable of. War and judgment and disintegrating flame. They will try to rip you to pieces. They don't want you whole."

I close my eyes, but lines still crisscross in my mind, sketching the broken shapes of Mom and Dad as they explode apart. The lines gouge deep into the surface of the earth like a net, fracturing land and water, pulling so tight that everything strains to implode, or maybe it's not the earth that's being squeezed but my head and my chest. I try to scream, but nothing happens. I try to claw my way out of this feeling, but Coyolxauhqui holds my hands still.

"But you, too, were born strong enough to fight. You don't have to let them break you. And you should never, never do the job for them. Do you hear me?"

I'm shaking, and I think I'm nodding, and bells are ringing and I'm being pulled in a thousand directions at once, and then I'm lying on the floor again and the kitchen is dark and empty and low-volume music crackles from the radio that blinks to switch from 12:00 to 12:01.

I stay in the kitchen until Mom comes out in her yellow cotton robe, grumbling about the alarm, and she sees me sitting on the floor with my knees pulled to my chest, and she's worried and she's sorry and she's half asleep, confused, her guilt pulling her apart.

I'm sorry for waking her, for hating her, for only hearing the anger and not the worry before. She's looking at me, hands on my face, my forehead, asking questions. My head is still spinning. My parents are still getting divorced. The world is still cracked in so many places, and the cracks on the side of my hand still throb. I don't know how to tell my mom what happened or what's happening to me. It seems impossible to begin. It seems pointless to try. I've been telling myself that there's nothing I can do to fix any of this.

But maybe I'm wrong. I still don't know if the world needs my voice. But I do.

I tell Mom I need help.

And she listens.

She listens when I say that everything is wrong. She shows me Ms. Delgado's email saying the same thing, suggesting counselors. She even tells me, weirdest of all, that she's felt it too. That she's talking to someone, that she's getting medication. I never knew that. She says she didn't know how to tell me.

When she finally helps me into bed, she kisses me twice, once on each cheek, and I swear, I hear bells.

I WANT TO GO HOME
by JUSTINE NARRO

I want to go home.

I can still see it, still feel it
The cuts and bruises on my knees,
the dirt under my fingernails,
and the sweat in my hair
from countless days and nights

of picking naranjas from my backyard tree

BBQs where I would go outside
to pick the chile piquín for the pico de gallo
and my tíos sat outside drinking Tecate and Modelo
while my dad cooked the fajita

of chasing light bugs

fireflies

lightning bugs

o luciérnagas, como dice mi abuelo

I want to go home.

A place you have never stepped foot on

but call it your land

A place you know nothing about

but say you have more right to

A piece of paper

and it is yours?

Because it is now "technically" legal

The gringos trick us

Promise us better

All for what?

To kill mi abuelo's abuelo

For a price

Because it is fair

Because it is now yours?

I want to go home.

The barrio where I was raised
A stucco home
with three bedrooms and one bath
Chickens and cabritos in the back
Our own natural lawn mowers

At five years old
when I helped place the now cracked tiles
in our new house

Where I swept the dirt off the concrete porch
not two inches above the ground
and played in the six-inch puddle of water on the edge of
the house,
where the land indented from years of our makeshift
driveway

I want to go home.

You say it is yours
because it is America's land
because it is on dirt
that is exactly the same on the other side of the river
with a different name

The cactus plants that housed the tortoises
The aloe vera that I would cut for sunburns
The leaves from the Mexican olive trees that I would collect

None of which you know how to use

I want to go home.

The place where I met every friend
My first day of school
and the boy next to me gave me a toothy grin
and ten years later asked me to prom

You say I don't belong
because it is your choice to make
where every memory is
where all my love is
where my life waits

I want to go home.

HOW TO EXIST IN A CITY OF GHOSTS
by **CAROLYN DEE FLORES**

How do I exist in a city of ghosts? By becoming one myself, of course.

I pull into my driveway after work. It takes twenty-five minutes to get here from Downtown San Antonio, so it is already past six in the evening, almost dark. I get out of my car, and a young boy, maybe eleven or twelve, comes speeding toward me on a BMX bicycle.

He stops in my yard and plants both feet on the sidewalk in front of my house. He stares at me with a defiant smile and tosses his head to flip the hair out of his eyes.

He watches me. I watch him.

Three houses away, behind the boy, an older woman, plump and wearing an apron, comes outside and waves her arms. She screams at the boy, yelling for him to come home, it's getting late.

The boy doesn't move. He doesn't hear her. Or, at least, he pretends not to hear her. He continues to stare at me. But I am not scared. The boy just wants my attention. He *dares* me not to notice him. He doesn't have to speak. He *has* a voice. I hear it loud and clear. The boy *demands* to be acknowledged. But I know what the boy really wants. He wants to feel more important than me.

I shrug to show him I see him. And that is enough.

The boy takes off, laughing and whooshing past me in a rush of wind. He is headed, of course, in the wrong direction.

I walk up to my house and turn the key. I am home.

~

It is one of those in-between years—

when you're an adult

and you're working

and you're making money

but you're still not quite responsible for anything but yourself.

~

You have that moment of being out of college, and having the big house but nothing to put in it. And you're still more concerned with things like going out on Friday and Saturday nights than you are with anything substantial. Although . . . going out on Friday and Saturday nights can be very substantial . . . when you're young.

Every night, every star, and every note is pregnant with possibility.

It is the year between depending on your parents' monthly

check so that you can even buy a pizza and renting your own home in the middle of some ghastly suburb where you know no one.

The chasm is a big one, and it's interesting to think that this is where most people's futures will be born. As for me, computer analyst by day, it is in *this house*, every night, that I become who I truly am. I smile to myself because *I am a composer.*

And starting out like this, filling up your house with all of the things you could never afford as a kid, most people would be surprised to find out that almost everything they work to become actually WILL happen.

Not because of good luck.

But because most people set the bar so low.

You see, it is into this world, a world where everything is either a disaster or a stupendous achievement, that occasionally a real awareness drips in.

Reality.

It makes its way down the streets of San Antonio . . . dripping, crawling . . . through downtown . . . over highways at night . . . under what used to be a railroad yard where somebody once stole a huge Indian archer shooting an arrow off the top of the railroad building . . .

Dripping still, through the dirty rain of retired businesses that will never be restored (unless through gentrification) . . . winding its way through the grass sitting at the edges of huge research facilities that are so secret (we really don't know what happens there) . . . through chain-link fences and barbed-wire enclosures . . . over highways . . . and a Suburban Park Mall (with lights that go on only at night when no one is actually shopping) . . . over that . . . and down the streets where dogs bark and echoes are heard by no one (except maybe other dogs and the occasional person who's been out too late drinking, walking home because they can't find their car) . . . down into what was (five hundred years ago) an open territory filled with life, hunting, and villages . . . down, down into a cul-de-sac, which no one will remember in the future (because people barely remember it now) . . . and makes its way, dripping, into the heart of a selfish, arrogant young whippersnapper like me.

———

I look at my living room full of rented furniture and one vanity that I bought at an antique store, and I go through the doors into the kitchen, which I only enter after I've been shopping for food to keep me alive. I can't even recall ever having eaten there . . .

Still, I go in, and it seems so cold, lifeless.

There's nothing there except for a spice rack someone gave me when I graduated.

It seemed like a weird gift then. It seems like an even weirder one now.

From all of this,

I take.

Huge.

Enjoyment.

I breathe it in—a sense of "I have arrived." Because when you're young and out of college, that's what it feels like.

I look at my kingdom, my empire.

The most perfect place imaginable because I turned it into a music studio! My band rehearses here.

There are keyboards stacked meticulously and cords organized by color. I did that myself.

And a drum set in the corner, of course, which reigns like a monarch on a throne.

Along one wall there are hundreds of CDs, all in alphabetical order by artist, and albums, too.

And that makes this, my house—my home—the epitome of accomplishment.

It feels pregnant with everything.

With possibilities. With fear. With the unknown. With everything but failure. Never failure.

Because at this point, how could *that* possibly happen?

But then comes this drip. It seeks me out—determined, persistent—streaming down the street, in the middle of the night, to *me*—even as *I* am more concerned with writing my first soundtrack for *City of Passion*, an independent movie.

I strike the first note on my 01/W keyboard, or maybe it's the D50 keyboard, and it's a good one. And I relish the fact that I am one of a handful of people in the city, or even in the surrounding cities, who really understands how to make music in this day and age.

I let it fill me. I let it swell. The tone pulses and reminds me of the sound of sirens in the city.

And I know I could never be happier than I am at this moment when I hit the second note . . .

~~~

Then the phone rings. I answer it. "Yes, Mother."

A few minutes later I go back to the keyboard. I jot down some notes about the song I am writing. I stop. I have a problem.

Am I sweating? I never sweat. As a matter of fact, I have one of those weird, weird diseases (I think) that does not enable you to sweat.

And I have to admit, at moments like this, in the middle of the night, when everyone else is asleep (I get very little sleep)—and I stand with my hands on the keyboard and feel the swell of the chord—my heart is open to possibilities and my head is open to the universe.

Except now, I can't stop thinking about one person.

A person I've never met.

A person I've never even heard of until today.

And to be quite frank, a person whose name I don't even know.

Today my mother told me about a lady who works at a hotel and found a wallet with five thousand dollars in it.

My mother interviewed her because my mother is a reporter. If the lady had kept the money, no one would have known. But she turned it in. That made it *news*.

My mother sat across the table from her, in one of the hotel rooms, and asked her, "So, how does it feel to have done something like this? Not everyone would have turned the money in."

My mother said the woman sat there, smiled, and told her,

"Oh, it is very exciting. *Everyone* has come to visit me. You're here. *You* came to visit me. *The TV people* came to visit me, and everyone is asking me questions!" The woman was thrilled at the attention.

Then the woman said, "You know, I've worked for thirty years at this same hotel. Every day, I do my best. I make the beds. I clean. I do extra just so that someone might notice. And every day, I put the little card where people can write their comments in the little placeholder on the stand. And then every day, *every day*, I wake up in the morning and I run in and I look at the card to see if anyone has written any comments.

"They never have. Ever. People leave me tips sometimes, but nobody has ever written a comment."

And, it makes me realize, standing in front of my keyboards, as I play these low notes—like wolves howling at the moon in the middle of the night—so many people live their lives with such nobility and no one ever notices them. Maids. Janitors. Gardeners. So many people in my city and in other cities around the world, who are good people and you never hear about them.

I hear my city of San Antonio scream with passion in the night, and it touches me. It is sad. It is sweet. It is *related*. I am a better person because I can hear it.

I play each note, and this theme song melts me. The sounds rise and fall with the pulse of my almost weeping city. And this woman's voice and all voices like hers join together in symphony.

I play the next note.

I finish my song. It is awesome.

And after that, I sit back and I close my eyes, pen in hand, and wait each night, listening for the ghosts in my city who scream out . . . and ask for nothing more than to be noticed . . . even if only once.

FILIBERTO'S FINAL VISIT
by FRANCISCO X. STORK

Sitting on the porch of the Cielo Vista Hospice, watching a freight train roll on and on. It's so long, people in cars waiting at the intersection are starting to turn off their engines and open windows. One guy is on his third cigarette. Then out of who knows where come the words that Filiberto Mendoza said to me some fifty years ago. "We Mexicans living in the US need to have dignidad."

I don't know why Filiberto's words come to mind just now. All I can think of is that these days I hear a lot about dying with dignity. I have a feeling the people who say that don't really know what dignity is. I think maybe all it means to them is that I should be able to go quietly, without too much pain. The more I think about dignidad, the more I know it's real and the less I know how to define it. One thing for sure is that Filiberto had it.

I met Filiberto when I was a freshman in high school. My

father had died the year before, and after the five thousand dollars in insurance money ran out, my mother and I moved into the Kennedy Brothers housing projects on the outskirts of El Paso. She went to work cooking breakfast and lunch for the Mt. Carmel Elementary School, and I got a speech scholarship to Jesuit High School.

I'll always remember Father Martinez, the priest at Mt. Carmel who helped me get that scholarship. After my father died, I started going to six o'clock Mass every morning. It was comforting to sit there in the dark old church. I felt less lonely. Me and maybe four old ladies showed up regularly. One day Father Martinez asked me to read the Epistles, and he saw that I was a good reader. I became a regular lector at the church, and eventually Father Martinez reached out to the school and helped me get that scholarship. That's pretty much what happened.

It was at Jesuit High where Louie Fresquez and I became friends. We were both on the speech team and each secretly wanted what the other had. Louie wanted my ability to speak in front of people and the trophies that came with that, and I wanted just about everything Louie had. He was the only freshman in the history of the school who had made it to the varsity basketball team. The first time I saw him, he had these expensive loafers, the kind with those little pom-poms. And his socks were so thin, they were transparent. I never imagined that we would become friends, me with my Kmart shoes and cheap white cotton socks, but we did.

Louie was seventeen and one of the few freshmen with a license. His parents bought him a used Mustang in good condition. I think Louie wanted to tell the world that he was not only good-looking and popular, but also on the way to being filthy rich. This is the same guy who knew he'd be a corporate lawyer when he was in kindergarten. The other thing you should know about Louie is that, even without the Mustang, he could, if he chose to, have a date with a different girl every Friday and Saturday night.

Yeah.

It was Louie who showed up with Filiberto one Saturday evening. I heard the honk and parted the living room curtain just enough to see a man with a shaved head and a white T-shirt sitting in the passenger seat of the Mustang. The man was in his early twenties and looked as if he had just gotten out of prison. There was something tattooed on the side of his skull, but I was too far away to read the words. The whole thing was enough, though, to give me an unsettled feeling in my gut that the entire evening was ruined, and I was pissed that Louie would throw a wrench in our carefully concocted plans for that Saturday night.

At sixteen my sex life was all wish and fantasy. That's why that Saturday evening was so important. I had some solid evidence that my solitariness would change that very night. I had met this girl at one of the speech tournaments. Her name was Patricia, but she asked everyone to call her Pita and not Patty. I thought she was attractive in her own way even though Louie said I was just desperate. What I liked about her was the suggestive way she spoke. There was always a hidden promise in her words. Not her words, exactly, but the way she said them. At the last speech tournament, she'd proceeded to tell me how her church was having a fair and how there was going to be a booth where you could get married to someone for an hour. They gave you a little plastic ring and an official-looking certificate, and you vowed to spend sixty minutes with each other, for better or for worse, in health or in sickness. I remember her pausing here for a moment to see if I had picked up on the implications of this. But I didn't. I'm sorry to say I was clueless. So she filled me in: "In back of the church there's a parking lot where the newlyweds go honeymoon."

The whole following week I was pretty much useless at school. I had to find a way to make it to that fair. It took some convincing, but I got Louie to give me a ride to the fair and to be my best man at the ceremony. I called Pita and she, as I'd hoped, was delighted with the idea of making the wedding even more realistic. She would get Louie a bridesmaid, no problem, and we were all set to roll.

But that Saturday evening, as I looked out the window, my meticulously imagined honeymoon suddenly felt in serious doubt. The guy sitting in the front seat with Louie did not seem like the marriage-booth type. Was he going to ruin this for me?

Louie honked again, so I closed the curtains and went to say goodbye to my mother. She made the sign of the cross on my forehead and said what she always said to me when I went out with Louie: "No hagas nada malo." I knew what she meant by "malo," and, sadly, it was beginning to look as if, in fact, I would not be doing anything malo on that particular night.

As I approached the car, I saw that the man in the passenger seat had rolled down his window and was smoking a cigarette. He did not turn to look at me in the back seat when Louie introduced us. His eyes were fixed on the group of kids sitting on lawn chairs, smoking pot and drinking beer on the playground across the street.

"Who are those guys?" Filiberto asked. "Some kind of gang?"

It took me a moment to realize the question was directed at me. "Oh. Um, they call themselves the Carnales," I said. "A gang, yeah. This housing project is their territory."

Filiberto turned around to look at me then. "You're afraid of them."

I wasn't sure whether this was a question or whether he was simply describing the obvious. What I knew for sure was that I was afraid of *him* at that very moment. I did my best to look him briefly in the eye and said, "I try to stay out of their way."

"How's that going?"

"All right. So far," I answered, ignoring what sounded like a tinge of disdain in Filiberto's voice.

"He poops in his pants every time he sees them," Louie said, trying unsuccessfully to be funny. Louie was not far from the truth, however. Those vatos were an ulcer-causing, stomach-churning pain in my day-to-day existence. Not only did I live in fear of them and of the way they looked at my mother, I also lived with the nauseating knowledge that I was a coward who peeked through closed curtains and looked around corners to make sure no Carnale was there. And when they whistled and shouted cat-calls at my mother, I walked on by as if I didn't hear them.

After a few moments of sizing me up in silence, Filiberto smiled. It was a smile and not a sneer, for which I was grateful. Then Louie started the car. Filiberto flicked his cigarette in the direction of the Carnales, not caring when a group of them stood and yelled as we sped away; I sunk deeper in my seat. I was suddenly filled with anger. Angry at Louie for ruining my evening and angry at this stranger who had just made my miserable life in the projects even worse than it was before. Filiberto's disrespectful gesture would come back to haunt me, of that I was certain.

I don't think I said a single word for the next twenty minutes. My anger subsided a little when I realized that we were still heading to the fair and there was still a possibility that the evening could be salvaged. I half listened to Louie asking Filiberto about his experience in Vietnam, where he had just returned from, and to Filiberto's monosyllabic answers.

"Did you ever engage in actual battle with the Vietcong?"

"Yes."

"What was it like?"

"Hell."

"Did you kill anyone?"

"Yes."

"How . . ."

"Ya. No más."

I was glad Filiberto didn't want to say more. I certainly didn't need to hear anything else.

When we got to the fair, Filiberto spotted the beer patio and headed there. The beer patio consisted of a dozen metallic tables inside a roped area. There was a sign near a tub of ice and a keg that said 21 OR OLDER. Next to the beer patio was a wooden stand where kids from a high school's mariachi band were blowing on their trumpets and tuning their guitars, getting ready to play. The whole front parking lot of the church was filled with booths for games and for selling every kind of food imaginable. Menudo, gorditas, tamales, tacos, and also corn dogs and pizza slices. There was even a booth called MexDonald's for those who preferred hamburgers with a touch of salsa. Kids were running around with cotton candy on their faces and teeth stuck to caramel apples. The whole scene was an instant mood lift. Even Filiberto seemed to have recovered from Louie's depressing interrogation. He bought five tickets from the man at the beer patio, pointed at a table, and said he would wait for us.

"Who's he?" I asked Louie as we searched for the much-anticipated marriage booth.

"He's a cousin. He's the son of the brother of my uncle's wife. Does that make him a cousin? He showed up at our house an hour before I had to pick you up. I didn't think he'd say yes when I asked him if he wanted to come." Then, after a pause: "Something's not right with him."

"As in the head?"

"He'll be normal and then poof, he's gone somewhere else. Or he'll flare up over nothing. Like in the car. I was just trying to have a conversation and then . . ."

"You were asking stupid questions."

"They weren't stupid. They were incisive questions."

"Incisive? Man, you don't have to be in lawyer mode all the time. You want to know what's incisive? Those guys he flipped his cigarette at. They'll *incise* me for sure when I get back."

"But at least you won't be a . . . virgin . . . when . . . you . . ."

I followed Louie's gaze and understood why Mr. Corporate Lawyer had stammered and was at a loss for words perhaps for the first time in his life. There, next to Pita, in front of the marriage booth, stood the young woman who was to be Pita's bridesmaid and Louie's partner. She was blonde, so blonde you almost had to shade your eyes. She was our age, yet she seemed like she had fully grown, while the rest of us were stuck as kids.

It amazes me now how much of what happened next I remember. I had seven dollars in my wallet, my mother's hard-earned money that I had taken earlier that day from her rent envelope. Those seven dollars, I learned quickly, were not nearly enough to pay for both the marriage ceremony and the customary post-wedding celebrations. The wedding was a dollar per participant, and I paid for Pita, of course. Then there was the Polaroid picture that would cement the occasion forever . . . and the heart-shaped frame—for a total of two dollars. I had just three dollars left by the time I saw Louie walk hand in hand with the bridesmaid in the direction of the Mustang. Pita wanted a celebratory dinner, and so off we went to the tamales tent. We had three tamales each: two dollars. I spent my last dollar trying to win a stuffed animal for Pita that she could "cuddle with" as she thought of me.

"Do you want to honeymoon?" I asked shyly as Pita hugged the red-and-blue stuffed parrot I had miraculously won for her.

"I need more time."

"But back at the speech tournament you said . . ."

"I didn't expect to fall for you. If I hadn't fallen for you, we could do it. But I fell for you."

"Oh."

I didn't know what to think. The way she said it and the way she looked at me, I knew she was telling the truth. Pita was feeling something serious and beautiful and I was stunned and baffled that someone could actually feel that way for me.

Pita grabbed my hand and pulled me toward the carousel, but I was broke and too embarrassed to tell her that I could not support her like a good husband should. I told her I had an older friend waiting for me at the beer patio, someone just back from Vietnam who was not well, mentally speaking, and I felt bad leaving him alone. She understood and urged me to go to my friend. I was instructed to call her that very night when I got home. Then she kissed me softly on the cheek. And so we parted ways. A temporary absence, in Pita's mind, and in mine, too, although I didn't realize it just then.

When I got close to the beer patio, I stopped and watched Filiberto. He seemed almost happy to be alone, smoking his Camels and sipping beer from a plastic cup. He hadn't gone "somewhere else" like Louie said. It was clear that he was very much here, engulfed by the blast of the mariachi trumpets and the smell of elotes roasting on a nearby grill. I stood there, not knowing where to go, until I saw him motion to me to come over and sit with him. He had a beer waiting for me when I got to his table. I glanced over at the old man working the keg, expecting him to come over and ask for my ID.

"Don't worry," Filiberto said. Then he looked at the old man and winked at him.

It was still a few years before I would acquire a taste for beer or alcohol. But I did not want to be disrespectful of Filiberto's offer, so I took a big gulp.

"The way to drink beer is to sip it. Make it last. That way you can enjoy it without getting drunk."

Just then a balloon popped next to us and Filiberto jerked his head nervously in the direction of the sound. I leaned over and tried to read the words tattooed on the side of his head.

Whom shall I fear?

"It's from the Bible," Filiberto said. He was looking at the little boy holding the limp string of the popped balloon, but somehow he knew I was reading his tattoo. He turned and faced me. "'The Lord is my light and my salvation, whom shall I fear?'"

"Psalm twenty-seven," I said. One of the Scriptures I often read at Mt. Carmel.

Filiberto nodded, smiled, and went silent. And just then, it did seem as if he had gone "somewhere else." What came to me while we were both quiet was that the only reason someone would tattoo the opening words of Psalm 27 on their skull was because they were facing a terrible opponent. The inner enemies that Filiberto was fighting had to be worse than even the Carnales, and yet, unlike me, he was not hiding from what he feared.

"It may be a while before we see Louie," I finally said. Then, mostly to myself, "Some guys have all the luck."

But Filiberto heard me. He looked at me with eyes that were

either full of kindness or full of pity. "How did it go for you?" I knew he was referring to my recent experience with matrimony.

I thought of cracking a joke, but there was something about the way he asked that invited honesty. "She said she had fallen for me, so she couldn't do it."

"Did she mean it?"

I thought for a few moments. "Yes."

Filiberto nodded. "So it was you who got lucky tonight."

"Me? Louie's out there . . ."

"I know what Louie's doing. I saw him walking to the car. What I'm telling you is that you got something tonight he didn't get."

"What?" I was truly interested in knowing because I had spent a lot of time thinking about all that Louie had, and all that I had in comparison, all that Louie was and all that I was, and I had always come out lacking.

Filiberto took a few deep breaths before he spoke again. "That girl who you were with, she had dignidad, man. Don't you see?"

I shook my head.

"Dignidad. It's something we Mexicans living here in the US need to have. We need to give value and worth to ourselves. Others won't give it to us. That girl you were with acted with dignidad tonight. She valued who she was. She valued *you*. She didn't want to cheapen what she felt. Not like those vatos back there where you live. They act all puffed like they're big stuff, but deep down they don't think they're worth anything. People look at them and then they believe none of us have any worth."

My memory of the rest of the night is very blurry after that. Despite Filiberto's advice, I gulped down the rest of my beer and another one, too. I remember Filiberto taking me to the churros tent and buying me a giant cup of coffee. After that we walked around, and when Pita saw us, she beamed at me in a way that I could now appreciate. And, I have to say, I was proud to be seen with Filiberto.

I never saw Filiberto again, except one time about a year later, when Louie showed up at school with an obituary from the *El Paso Times*. Filiberto Mendoza, twenty-two years, of Socorro, Texas, died instantaneously when his truck was struck by an outgoing freight train at the intersection of North Loop and Zaragoza.

One day, shortly after that, Joey, the little brother of one of the Carnales, came up to me as I was walking home and asked me if it was true that the vato who protected me was dead.

"What?"

"The bald dude with the tattoo on his head. He came over one day and told my brother that if anything happened to you or your family, they'd have to deal with him."

The catcalls and menacing stares had stopped a while back. I had been grateful without letting myself wonder why. Now I knew.

"What's going to happen now?" I asked Joey.

"Nobody cares about you. You're a piece of mierda."

Except that by then I had been going out with Pita for a year and she had convinced me that I wasn't. Filiberto was right. I had found my dignidad.

COCO CHAMOY Y CHANGO

by e.E. CHARLTON-TRUJILLO

Only when the bottle spins do I remember . . .

I had this dream of Frida Kahlo painting a picture of me naked with my heart on my sleeve and my stomach in my hands. Mama shouts to me from my sister's kitchen, saying I need to take out the trash before my dad gets home. Only, in the dream, I know he's not coming home because he never does. I also know that my sister doesn't have a kitchen with Talavera tile floors and yellow plaster walls because she died in the womb with me, but my mind has made up the kitchen (and my sister) all the same.

I salivate from the smell of flour tortillas warming on the comal. The rolling, low boil of Mama's spicy Spanish rice rumbles along the walls, shaking the floors. Frida doesn't care. She keeps painting me naked even though I'm standing in her Casa Azul studio with my baggy boy jeans and a wrinkled blissful-blue button-down. Frida can see through my clothes. She can see through my tousled hair, dripping over the right side of my crooked face. She can see through everything

I'm scared to say out loud because she's Frida fucking Kahlo. And just before I wake up, I hear—

"Daniela." Ruben nods toward the bottle. "Truth or dare?"

I hear the sound of crying and realize it's me. It's me that's crying in the dream . . .

And I still hear it even in a basement booming with hip-hop—full of people I don't really know at a party I didn't want to come to. Sitting in a circle playing spin the bottle because everyone is horny or bored or some kind of both, I guess.

"¿Qué pasa?" Ruben says.

The laughter and music crackle—ache in my right ear. I don't want a truth or a dare. I don't want this circle of juniors and seniors and even people who graduated back in May to stare at my broken face.

Ruben leans in, whispers, "Just pick."

I stare at the bottle of Mexican Coke, pointing its chipped glass lip at me from the shiny auburn concrete floor. I clear my throat, "Um. Dare, I guess," because *truth* would be impossible.

"Órale," Jorge shouts from across the circle. "Taco Bell Mexican is in for a dare."

"Cut it out," CoCo says to him.

"Ay, I was just messing with her."

"*Them,*" she corrects.

Marisol "CoCo Chamoy" Hernández's gaze falls loosely in my direction. The reflection of dangling Christmas lights glistens in her eyes—soft, insistent. There are at least seven hundred and seventy-seven poems waiting to be written in them. All about change and revolution. About the institution of injustice and oppression. She fears nothing. I fear everything.

"Seven minutes in heaven with CoCo Chamoy!" Ruben announces.

Howls boom! Clapping breaks out. I cover my right ear from all the noise.

"Wait—what?" I say.

I look at CoCo. The poems have vanished from her eyes. Replaced with the uncomfortable feeling of being locked in a—

"Closet! Closet! Closet!" roars out from a few.

"They can't go in there," Jorge says to Ruben.

"Ay, Mexican. You didn't care when you stuck me and Pablo in there last summer." Ruben stands up. "Rules are rules."

"It's fine." CoCo steps over the bottle, pulling me up off the floor.

I look at her.

She looks at me.

The edges of the basement, all of the people in it drop away for one brief yet elongated second. I pretend in this sweeping break in time that Frida is standing there, painting CoCo and me. That we can belong on her canvas and—

"Let's go." Ruben ushers us past the air hockey table and throwback arcade of Pac-Man gobbling Pac-Man bits.

Ruben unlocks the closet door, grinning like I've never seen.

"I don't want to do this," I tell him. "Seriously."

"You said dare." He pushes me into the closet. "Besides, it's just ten minutes."

"You said seven—"

He shuts the door fast. The lock clicks into place.

"Ruben!" I wait, staring at the faint, fogging glow of light through the bottom of the door. Nothing.

"It goes by fast." CoCo's round, rich voice trails through the darkness. "I've been in three times."

"I don't like to be locked . . . in places," I say.

Even if it is with the infamous CoCo.

The flashlight on CoCo's cell sprays across the ceiling. Steep shadows climb the walls. All around us, shelves and shelves of plastic bins, labeled and stacked. Folded clothes, boxes of sneakers. An entire pallet of toilet paper. Two shelves of detergent. So much—

"I could fit my whole bedroom in here." She flashes the light along the clear sides of the bin. "The one-stop, bulk-buy treasure trove. Bottled water, black beans, pens, pills, tampons, Tajín. Doritos and Takis for days. If the apocalypse is upon us, we're ready."

I grin.

"You have a nice smile," she says, digging into a bin of chips.

What does CoCo Chamoy know about me smiling? About me and anything? We are shapes shifting, shuffling, mostly rushing through the high school hallways. We are unmet glances during pep rallies, football games, and awkward school dances. She's the one leading protests against gun violence and kids caged along the border while me? Really, I'm just trying to keep my head above water.

She pops open a bag of Doritos, facing it toward me. "You should do it more. Smile."

Self-consciously, I turn the right side of my face away from her. Knowing it's just lying there . . . torcida, muted and dead.

Someone pounds on the door, giggles. The shadows of foot-steps soon peel away.

"I wasn't going to come," she says, selecting her chip with precision. "Tonight."

"Me neither. Ruben's mom made him invite me."

"Don't the two of you go back?" she asks.

"A long way back. Now it's 'qué pasó' and head nods like we're bros. We're definitely not bros."

I lean against the cement wall, the coolness expanding across my warm back. I start to relax until I see her watching me, my face. I shift into the shadow of my hair, falling forward. Wanting to be invisible. Wanting this to be over.

"Freshman year," she says "I ended up in here with Toby Anderson. Ruben's parents had just moved in, so less snacks. More random boxes piled everywhere. The two of us crouched by the door. We moaned and pounded on boxes. Really over-the-top."

I attempt a grin. The left side of my face trembles, so I stop.

"Sophomore year," she says, "I got stuck with some gringo from the Valley. That was weirder." She pauses. "He was a no-means-maybe kind of guy. I texted Alizae to get me out of here. And she busted in fast. She was like baboso this and pinche that. I think she scared the creep right out of him."

"I'd believe that," I say quietly.

"She says you make the best mangonada. At your aunt's fruitería. Alizae's kind of a mangonada connoisseur, so I have to think they're pretty good."

I shrug.

"She said she didn't see you there all summer," CoCo says. "How come?"

I shrug, again because I don't know what to tell her, but there she is, waiting for me to say something.

"I just wasn't," I say.

"Same. I mean, I wasn't around. I was at my sister's in Austin. You ever go?"

I shake my head.

"Oh, you have to," she says. "It's the best city in Texas. I'm moving there the second I graduate. You can be anything in Austin. Not like here. You know?"

Stabbing quiet crawls between us. I'm in seven minutes in heaven and feeling like it's ten minutes of hell because I can't just—

"Did I do something?" she asks.

"I just." I clear my throat. "I don't always know what to say . . . to people."

She returns my shyness with a half smile. "Tell me something. Like . . . what's your favorite thing on the menu? At the fruitería?"

A trunk of fruits and flavors spills across my mind. A tickle for tangy, tart tamarind wraps half the width of my tongue. The smooth-coolness of shaved ice with pickle juice and tiger's blood, cucumber slices and watermelon chunks. There's one thing, though . . . that's my favorite. I just can't say it. Not to her.

I wedge alongside crates of Coke and sit down. "Um . . . our corn cups with crushed Flamin' Hot Cheetos are pretty good."

The sound of booing spears along the edges of the door. The music changes. Country.

CoCo's phone chimes. She shakes her head, reading it. "Jorge says I should be careful around you. You might turn me gay. As if that's how it works, right?"

I don't say anything. Just rub my thumb over a jagged groove on the floor.

"I think it's cool," she says. "That you're not afraid to be you. To be into girls. To—"

"What?"

"It's okay." She closes the bag of chips. "You and Zoe Hills."

"That never happened. That was asshole homophobes like Jorge making shit up." I shift uncomfortably. "I don't know . . . what I'm into."

Which is a lie. I know exactly what I'm into. What I think about, ache for. I look at CoCo. Her eyes see through me. Kind of like Frida. Only now there is nowhere to go—to hide.

"I made out with a girl," she says, sitting down.

I chuckle. "On a dare."

"No. We hooked up after a rally in Austin."

I gulp. Can't believe she's serious.

"I liked it," she says. "How soft her lips were. The way her hands held on to my waist. It's just different. You know?"

I don't know, because kissing and touching have only been sketched in the wildness of my imagination.

"Then why are you with Jorge?" I ask.

"He's not a bad guy."

"He's not a good one either."

"Why can't you say if you like girls?" she asks.

I wait for her to answer for me, but she doesn't.

"When I told my mom I made out with a girl . . ." She pauses, then: "She just said, 'Ay, mija. That's such a hard life.' But the next day, she said, 'I love you.' Asked if I was okay. That was it. No big drama. No burning in Hell. No anything bad. Just 'I love you. Are you okay?' That's how it's supposed to be, you know? That simple."

"Five minutes!" Ruben shouts through the door.

"What did your mom say when you told her that you're into girls?" she asks.

"I didn't say I was."

"You didn't say you weren't."

"Why is this, like, so important to you?" I ask. "It's not as simple as do I like girls or guys or whoever."

"That's fair. I mean. Love is political. Faith, war, gentrification, fucking dress code is political."

"I don't know that I'm trying to be political—make a statement."

"Your existence is a statement, Dani. There's no one person like you in this town. You don't assimilate to fit the mold. I wish I were more like that sometimes."

I laugh.

"What?" she says.

"You're Marisol 'CoCo Chamoy' Hernández. Junior class president. State finalist in debate. You lead protests. You challenge racist, misogynistic teachers like Mr. Reynolds, knowing he'll tank your grade for it. Pues, for real, that's making a statement. I couldn't do that."

She doesn't say anything. Just sits there, studying me. I want to ask her what she's thinking—what are the images and the sounds. ¿Qué colores? What is the brush she paints me with?

"Now I feel like I said something wrong," I say.

CoCo crawls over, sits across from me. The tips of her boots press against my sneakers. It's electric, the energy of her proximity. I don't know what to do with it—with her—so close.

"Imagine you're at the movies in the city, okay?" she says. "Big stadium theater full of people, and it catches fire. Flames screaming up the walls. Now, do you sit there and just watch it burn?"

"No. I do something. I . . . get people out."

"What if they hate you—fear you?" she says. "Just for being you."

"One, that's stupid because everything's on fire, right? They don't got time to hate me. And even if they called me Taco Bell Mexican because of my pale-ass skin, I'd help 'em. You can't just let people burn."

"Exactly." She leans forward. "See, you get it. How many of them on the other side of the door even notice the walls are burning? Like, really see it? What's happening in our community? This country? The systems in place don't just make space for racism. They perpetuate it. In school. Along the border. But we come to Ruben's parties on the last day of summer. We cannonball in the pool or jump on the trampoline. We spin the bottle so we don't have to think."

"It's a lot," I say. "Sometimes it's just easier to Snapchat and scroll for people. There's only so much you feel like you can do."

She shrugs. "I don't know. I feel like if I just scroll and click out—I'll burn with the walls. Like with my brother. He used to see how things were connected. How injustice was connected. Now he's like, 'My back ain't wet. They're not coming for me.' He's nothing but ash. I don't want to be like that. Turn my back on my culture—on what's real. Just . . . disappear."

"Pues, you could never disappear, CoCo. It's kinda like with clouds, right? Even if they filled up the whole sky, tornado dark, you always know the sun is right behind them. Waiting."

Her face softens, her eyes lighter. "So I'm like the sun."

I drop my eyes to the floor. "You're like a dozen of them."

I tip my head toward her, unable to hold more than a glance. My stomach twists, travels to the bottom of my feet.

"How come we've never talked before?" she says. "Just . . . talked."

I grin. "We did. Once. Kind of."

"When?"

"Third grade," I say. "I'd broken my leg in two places. It was so bad. I came to school with this cast way up to my crotch almost. I couldn't really do anything at recess but sit. Watch everybody. You came by. Asked me where I broke it. I pointed here." My lower leg tingles. "You drew this little cartoon monkey."

"Chango." Her smile pries open my heart. "I made him up when I was a kid. I used to draw him on everything. Make these little comics. *Aventuras de CoCo y Chango.*"

"You said he would look out for me. That he always did for

you. So when they cut the cast off," I say, "I asked if I could keep that part of it, but they sawed him down the middle. Split him in half."

Something quiet and serious settles into her.

"Dani . . . what happened? With your face."

I immediately want to sink into the floor.

"I'm sorry, I—" she says. "You just . . . seem so uncomfortable."

I can't look at her. I can't run from her. I'm just here. Stuck. Nowhere to go when she touches my knee.

"Hey," she says.

"It's, um . . . this thing. Bell's palsy. Basically your face just . . . freezes. On one side."

My exhale is shaky.

"Does it hurt?" she asks.

"No. I mean, mostly not. I get tired sometimes because the right side doesn't move. My right ear kind of bugs me. Sort of like an earache that doesn't go away."

She stays quiet. Polite quiet. Freaked quiet. Some kind of quiet that reminds me of my mom when we went to the ER and first found out.

"It's supposed to go away," I say.

"Okay."

"That's what they keep telling me. The doctors—that it'll go away."

"That's good."

I pull my knees to my chest, rest my chin against them.

"Can you feel things?" she asks.

"Not on the frozen side."

"That would scare the shit out of me."

I laugh. "Yeah. It did. It still does sometimes. I never thought about my face before except how much I hated it. My mom always trying to take pictures of me, and I was like, 'Stop already.' Now I just . . . What if doesn't go back? Like before."

"But they think it will?"

"Yeah," I say.

"What about your mouth?"

"The part that's numb feels heavy. Like fat or something."

She reaches out. I flinch at first, but then watch her gently brush her fingers against my lips. My heart races as she stumbles across them.

"They don't feel heavy or fat," she says, stopping. "They feel like lips."

Fists pound against the door. "Two minutes!" Ruben shouts.

CoCo stands up, lifting bin lids, digging through several of them before sitting back down. She uncaps a Sharpie, turns over my palm, and pauses.

"Azul?" she says, looking at my hand.

Traces of dry ocean-blue paint pour from a crease between two of my fingers.

"I was painting," I say. "My aunt's spare room."

CoCo's hand lingers just above mine before her fingertip follows the longest line of my palm. Not holding my breath is so hard because this feeling—of her touching me—it's nothing like I would've imagined. Real touch feels exciting and scary and amazing.

She reaches the bottom of my palm and pauses at my wrist.

"Let's pretend"—she steadies the tip of the marker along my skin—"that Chango and I are on an adventure."

My eyes trail along the black lines taking shape. Quickly, they become eyes, ears, a nose—their alignment out of sync because Chango is winking. My own eyes follow from my hand and beyond the sacred heart medallion floating in midair around CoCo's neck, past the smallest of scars along her chin to her—

"What do you think?" She tilts her head, eyeing my palm.

She's still holding my hand when I look back down at it.

"Y-yeah," I stammer.

And there we are. Me looking at her. Her looking at me. Where all the noise on the other side of the door fades. Where all the fear inside me cools. Where I imagine Frida standing in the corner, painting us dreaming in sapphire—in nothing but bold blues.

"I really think you have a nice smile," she says.

My heart has now joined my stomach at the bottom of my feet. The contraction of air between us—the push, the pull, the expansion of shallow light and deep shadows narrowing.

Her lips part, and before I can say something, the door swings open.

Our hands drop.

"CoCo," says Jorge. "Let's go."

Her pained eyes reach inside my chest and hold on so tight. I fight the urge to look away, trying to find a way to make this moment with CoCo last longer.

"He's yours," she says. "Until you wash him away."

She gets up, and before I can manage words into a sentence, she's gone. I stare at my open palm. At the blue line of paint running along Chango's face. Splitting him in half.

I never want to wash him away.

TELL ME A STORY/DIME UN CUENTO

by XAVIER GARZA

Tell me a story.

Dime un cuento.

It can be a long story, or it can be a short one too.

It can be a brand-new cuento, or a favorite old one.

You can tell me the story of how as a kid you used to play with canicas. Tell me cuentos of these magical marbles made of glass that sparkled with every color of the rainbow when you held them up to the sun.

You can tell me a scary story. You can tell me the cuento of how el Chupacabras is lurking outside my window, waiting to make me its next victim!

You can tell me a happy story. Like the cuento of how as a kid you liked seeing Grandma dance merengue songs with Grandpa.

But just don't tell me a sad story. Because sad cuentos always make me cry.

You can tell me a Christmas story. You can tell me the cuento of Santa's Mexican cousin who delivers presents to all the good little boys and girls who live along both sides of the US and Mexico border.

You can tell me a story of the heroes of la lucha libre, Papa. Tell me cuentos of these masked heroes and villains who wear shiny capes.

You can tell me a story about Mexico. You can fill my head with cuentos of its grand fiestas, colorful piñatas, leyendas, beautiful music, and sweet-tasting paletas. Better yet, why not make the story be a bilingual cuento and tell it to me in both English and Spanish? Why not give me the best of both worlds?

Just tell me a story. Dime un cuento. Tell it to me as I close my eyes and go to sleep.

Tell me a story. Dime un cuento.

MY NAME IS DOLORES
by GUADALUPE RUIZ-FLORES

On the first day of school, I trembled as the teacher walked toward me. Her clunky shoes made a loud noise on the worn wooden floor. I clutched my brand-new red tablet to my chest. All eyes turned toward me.

She came closer. I stiffened and drew back as she bent her full figure over my desk. Everyone called her Mrs. Collins, so I knew that was her name. Her face came within inches of mine, so close that I could smell her perfume. Words formed on her lips. English words that I didn't understand.

Her hair was combed back into a neat, tight bun, reminding me of Aunt Celia. It shimmered like gold. I wanted to reach out and touch it. Instead my fingers gripped the tablet even tighter as she asked me something in a language I didn't speak. The words came so fast, my mind reeled.

¿Qué dice, Maestra? I blurted out in Spanish before I could think. *What are you saying, teacher?* She tilted her head to one

side, as if confused, her eyebrows coming together over the bluest eyes I had ever seen.

The night before, I had asked Papi, "What do I say when the teacher speaks to me in English? I won't understand."

"You will. You've picked up a few words of English over the summer," he said.

I frowned. "Just a few. But what if she asks me something really hard?"

He paused momentarily, deep in thought. "Just say, 'I don't know. My name is Dolores.'"

I looked at him blankly.

"She will probably only be asking for your name, that's all," Papi assured me.

"What if she asks something else?"

"You just repeat what I told you," he said. "She'll understand that you're still learning the language."

"But, Papi, what if I need to use the toilet?"

"Just say 'Bis'cuse me, please,'" he replied. "That way the teacher will excuse you."

I hope I can remember all this. "But, Papi," I said, "what if I forget?"

"Ay, Dolores. You worry too much," he said with a chuckle. "You'll be fine."

But I couldn't stop worrying. Later that night, as I snuggled under the thin quilt in the bed I shared with my sister, Oralia, I kept rehearsing Papi's words. *I don't know, my name is Dolores; I don't know, my name is Dolores; I don't know . . .*

Sitting in the classroom for the first time, staring into Mrs.

Collins's eyes, I remembered Papi's words. I leaned forward and whispered to her. "I don't know. My name is Dolores." I searched her face for some indication that I had given the right answer. There was none.

Maybe I didn't say it right. "I don't know. My name is Dolores," I repeated quite loudly. The teacher looked confused. She asked me something again.

My jaw tensed. I curled my toes inside my shoes in frustration. "I don't know. My name is Dolores," I said meekly for the last time.

Muffled sounds filled the classroom and swept like a gentle wave coming in from the sea. At first, just a murmur. Then the sound grew louder and louder. The girls whispered and giggled. The boys pointed and sneered. Struggling to hold back tears, I slumped farther down in my chair. My face felt hot, like it had the time I got too close to the woodstove while Mami was cooking.

"Shhhh," the teacher said to the students. The class got quiet. She turned back to me and asked something again. This time I just shrugged and lowered my eyes so she couldn't see my tears.

~

Weeks passed. I still hadn't made any friends, but I found out the red-haired girl with the freckles was Lucy. The one with the blonde curls was her friend Cassie. They always played jump rope at recess. I sat on a bench and watched.

The boys snickered when the teacher called on me and I'd stumble over my words. The more they laughed, the madder I got. I'd show them I wasn't dumb. I paid attention to how the teacher formed her words. I repeated them silently in my head. I wrote and rewrote each word that was on the board in my tablet. I studied its meaning and spelling.

But sometimes things didn't make sense. Like when the teacher called a manzana an apple and a plátano a banana. I couldn't believe words could sound so different in English and Spanish and mean the same thing. Every time I learned a new word in English, my excitement mounted.

One day Mrs. Collins announced that we were having our class picture taken the following week. "Dress in your best Sunday clothes," she said.

Mami was as excited as I was. The night before the picture taking, she washed and dried my thick black hair with a towel.

"Your first school picture," she said, curling my hair for the next day. "You have to look good." She hummed as she took long strands of my hair, rolled them in curlicues, and plastered them against my skull with bobby pins. She starched and ironed a yellow polka-dot dress bought at the church rummage sale. She hung it carefully on a nail on the wall.

"We don't want it to wrinkle."

She took out the same white silk bow I had worn the first day of school and placed it on the kitchen table.

"So we don't forget to pin it on tomorrow," she said.

The next morning, Mami unrolled my long black curls. They cascaded like a waterfall down my shoulders. She pinned the bow on top of my head. I felt like a princess. I flipped my curls from side to side just to show off.

When I got to school, I was glad I had dressed up. Some girls wore dresses with flower prints. Others wore pleated skirts and white cotton blouses with dainty buttons. Many wore bows in their hair. Most of the boys wore white shirts and dark pants.

Right before lunch, Mrs. Collins said, "All right, everyone. Time to go outside and get our picture taken."

We lined up by rows in front of the steps of the three-room schoolhouse. The taller ones stood in the back. The teacher sat in the front row, looking very pretty in her pink-flowered dress.

"Don't forget to smile for the camera when I tell you," the photographer said as he adjusted his tripod and looked through his camera.

I was short and in the front row, standing between Arnold and Jerry, the two shortest boys in the class. I smiled my biggest smile. Suddenly something happened. The photographer called Mrs. Collins over. They talked for a minute. They both looked at me. Goose bumps went up and down my body. I started fidgeting. Had I done something wrong?

I was stunned when Mrs. Collins took me firmly by the arm and led me to the side, away from the group, away from the camera's view.

"You wait here, dear," she said, pointing to a bench nearby. She rushed back and sat in the front row with her students. "Go ahead." She smiled. "We're ready."

The photographer nodded. Within a few minutes, it was over. We all hurried inside. Everyone took their seats and got their lunches. I couldn't eat mine. My stomach hurt like the time I ate too much candy and threw up.

The rest of the day was a blur. I stared at the railroad tracks across the road, thinking about the picture. I must have done something wrong. Was my dress not pretty enough? Was my bow on crooked? I looked at my worn shoes with the tips that looked like canoes. They were hand-me-downs from my cousin Consuelo. That was it! The kids were always making fun of my shoes. It must have been the ugly shoes. I tried to hide them, pushing my feet farther under my desk.

When I got home, I told Mami what had happened. Her smile disappeared. She helped me out of my dress, hung it carefully on the nail, but not before I saw tears running down her cheeks.

"THERE ARE MEXICANS IN TEXAS?"

How Family Stories Shaped Me

by **TRINIDAD GONZALES**

I was getting lunch at L'Enfant Plaza in Washington, DC, when a worker at the café told me, "Go back to where you came from." My response of "Texas" prompted a befuddled "There are Mexicans in Texas?"

I smirked. "Yes, there are Mexicans in Texas." I left without offering a history lesson and returned to eat my lunch at the Smithsonian Institution's Center for Folklife and Cultural Heritage housed in the same building.

Sitting in my cubicle, I listened to the chitchat between my two advisors, Olivia Cadaval and Cynthia Vidaurri. Olivia, originally from Mexico City, and Cynthia, from Robstown, Texas, guided me through the world of DC and the Smithsonian. I was living away from the comfort and familiarity of the Lower Rio

Grande Valley of Texas for the first time, and both ladies helped me navigate the polite, bureaucratic world of racism that liberal institutions such as the Smithsonian can harbor. The Center for Folklife would become one of my havens, regardless of how far I was from home and all its traditions.

My father was always the one both sides of my family requested to barbecue, and through those countless barbecues, I learned the art. From an early age I studied how to know when mesquite was ready to be burned (too green, stinky meat), and how to build a fire with the principle of patience and wind. Brasas, embers, for cooking take time to make. Barbecue in South Texas represents familial and community bonding. As I age, the smell and crackle of burning mesquite invokes in me a nostalgic, safe space—sometimes happy and sometimes sad.

During the hours of building a fire, seasoning the meat, and slow cooking, my father—the family historian—told me stories about our family. These stories were meant to remind me of where and from what gente, people, I came from. My family traces its ancestry to the Spanish colonization of the area that began in 1749 and includes Apache lineage. The Spanish settlers were ranchers, and my ancestors on both sides of my family were vaqueros, cowboys. My ancestors' stories, along with my father's and mother's stories, shaped me in ways I did not understand at the time. But these stories would help me navigate the rude racism of the street later in life.

During the summer of 1976, we celebrated the Bicentennial in the All-American City of Edinburg, Texas. A celebration that united us as Americans. My father bought a wood-carved bald eagle that hung in our living room. The eagle held a draping United States flag through its beak and claws as if it were in flight, and hung from a plank that had 1776 branded on it. We had just moved into our home on Garza Street, and I was going to attend the newest elementary school in town, Freddy Gonzalez. I was excited because the school was named for Alfredo Cantu "Freddy" Gonzalez, who had received the Medal of Honor for his heroic deeds during the Tet Offensive of the Vietnam War. Coming from a military family, it was hard not to know about Freddy Gonzalez as a local and national hero. But he was not the only one from Edinburg to die during the war; fourteen others lost their lives serving as well, and my father reminded me that was one of the highest percentages of casualties for a community our size.

By 1970 there were only a little over seventeen thousand people living in my hometown. I was a proud Mexican American kid, and I thought that all Americans were essentially like me, with some differences in the foods we ate, our looks, language, and names. To me, Edinburg was small-town America with apple pie and fajitas, George Jones and Country Roland Band. It was Tex-Mex, but all-American.

One of my first memories attending Freddy Gonzalez was being told that an older white teacher did not like Mexicans and that she would pinch you if you spoke Spanish. While the Chicana/o Movement of the 1960s and early 1970s helped end the official practice of punishing students for speaking Spanish, individual teachers would continue it. I remember when my friend said something to me in Spanish on the walkway outside of class and this teacher reached down to pinch him. I can still see his facial reaction of pain. Childhood trauma remains with us like ghosts. We either tame it or allow it to haunt us. Sometimes I guess it is both. This was the first time I sensed we were different. The first time I ever experienced such a feeling.

A story told several times by my dad was about his experience in the army while stationed in Germany. It was the early 1960s, and he made both Black and white friends. One day, while walking with his friends in the mess hall, a white soldier told him, "Go back where you came from, wetback." My father's friends wanted to start a fight, but my dad held them back with his arm and said, "No. He is right. I am a wetback." He then turned to the racist soldier and said, "Here in Europe, I am a wetback, but when we return to the United States, you are the wetback because I am Indian." The racist soldier did not know how to respond, and my dad's friends laughed. I did not grow up raised as a Native American, but my father made sure I never forgot that besides being Mexican, we had Lipan Apache heritage as well.

The stories my mother told me centered on her migrant farmworker experiences during the late 1940s and 1950s. She talked about picking cotton and how her father ran crews north following the seasonal picking circuit in Texas. One of the stories she liked to tell was when my aunt Piedad, who at the time was in her early teens, went into a segregated restaurant in Robstown and asked for ice cream. My aunt was light skinned and passed as white, so the waitress served her. When my mom and my aunt Minerva walked in and started talking to Piedad, the waitress asked who her friends were. Piedad responded that they were her younger sisters and wanted ice cream too. My mother would imitate the surprised look the waitress made because my mom and Minerva were dark skinned and could not pass as white. The embarrassed waitress served them ice cream as well, but they all had to sit away from the other customers. My mom would always laugh when she told this story because the waitress felt compelled to serve little Mexican girls. She felt like they pulled a fast one in segregated Texas during the early 1950s.

But there's another story my mother never told me, about her speaking Spanish to her friend as they waited in line at Luby's, when a Winter Texan, a Midwestern/Northern retiree who resided in the LRGV during the winter, told my mother to speak English. She turned to the Winter Texan and said in English that she could speak whatever language she wanted and to mind his own business.

My mother didn't tell me this story herself. She was talking to her friends and sisters during merienda, afternoon coffee and sweet bread. I was listening to the adults talk as I ate my empanada or marranito. By this point, I was aware of racists' views concerning Mexican Americans and speaking Spanish. But this was no longer just a feeling of being different. It was a feeling of knowing that we were viewed as different and that some people did not see us as American. This fact was clear by fifth grade, and growing up meant just dealing with it. Scholars would later call this "adoption grit." But for racial minorities, it was called learning to live in America.

~~~~~~

By the time I worked at the Smithsonian in 1999, things were beginning to change. Or so I thought. I was the first Latino co-op student-employee, a position created by the Secretary of the Smithsonian as part of the institution's response to its lack of Latinx representation in its exhibits, collections, curators, and staff. In 1994 the Smithsonian Institution Task Force on Latino Issues produced "Willful Neglect: The Smithsonian Institution and U.S. Latinos." The report states, "The Smithsonian Institution, the largest museum complex in the world, displays a pattern of willful neglect towards the estimated 25 million Latinos in the US." The report further states, "Many Smithsonian officials project the impression that Latino history and culture are somehow not a legitimate part of the American experience. It is difficult for the Task Force to understand how such a consistent pattern of Latino exclusion from the work of the Smithsonian could have occurred by chance."

As part of the co-op position, the University of Texas–Pan American, now UT Rio Grande Valley, paid me to do fieldwork for the Center for Folklife's El Río program. I interviewed possible participants for the annual Smithsonian Folklife Festival.

I translated and transcribed the interviews to help develop the program and for future scholars to read. The Center for Folklife produces the annual festival during the two weeks leading up to the July Fourth celebration at the National Mall. The festival highlights a state and/or region of the United States, as well as a foreign nation. It is a living museum where culture bearers share their community's history and traditions with audience members through cooking sessions (called foodways), music events, and set programing on stages to discuss topics or issues. It was an inclusive experience like no other I had encountered before and one that I would find elusive at times in DC and the rest of the Smithsonian.

The first week I lived in DC, Cynthia allowed me to stay with her while I looked for an apartment. In DC it is common for people to share a house where individuals pay rent for a room and split the utility costs. Before smartphones, apps, and Craigslist, people advertised looking for roommates through classified ads in newspapers and magazines. The first day I stayed at Cynthia's house, I sat in her living room, making calls and leaving messages inquiring about renting a room. It was an exciting time, as I anticipated meeting new people and living in the national capital while working at the Smithsonian Museum, our nation's museum.

After three or four days of calling, I never received a response. I began to grow desperate. It was becoming clear that someone named Gonzales was not going to get a callback in DC, and I needed to move out because I did not want Cynthia to think I was taking advantage of her hospitality. Cynthia lived in Columbia Heights, next to Mount Pleasant, the Latinx part of DC. I decided to walk to nearby apartment complexes, vertical buildings—not sprawling units like in Texas—to try my luck in finding a place. As I wandered, I came across the Woodner Apartments and stepped into the lobby. The mix of people from around the world and the multiple languages spoken— English, Spanish, and Somali, to list just a few—was a welcome chorus to the silence that I had initially received from DC. I was immediately welcomed.

The Woodner Apartments became my refuge, like it had been for working-class African Americans during the 1970s and, later, immigrants from around the world. Over two thousand people live in the Woodner on a regular basis. While the Center for Folklife was a racially and ethnically diverse space within the Smithsonian, the reality was that the rest of the Smithsonian staff, curators, and management was not diverse in 1999. The National Museum of the American Indian (2004) and the National Museum of African American History and Culture (2016) did not exist at the time. Returning to the Woodner after work brought me to a world of sound and smells that filled a void.

Dinnertime became my favorite part of the day. As I made my way through the lobby and up the elevator, then walked the hallways to my efficiency, I would take in the smells of spices people used to cook dishes from their native Africa, Latin America, and other parts of the world and the United States. My addition to those smells was cooking charro beans, and arroz con pollo with a heavy hand of comino. The smells of cooking reminded me that I was part of the world that had migrated to DC. America was more than the silence I had initially received; America was a home the world came to to live better lives, and that America is us.

~~~

The power to represent people and their communities that rests with the Smithsonian is impressive because people view its exhibits and programing as authoritative. In 2018 alone more than twenty-eight million people walked through Smithsonian museums and institutions. Taking care to make sure exhibits and programming follow scholarly standards and respect is important because people look to the institution to tell our nation's history and explain the diverse cultures that compose the United States. At the Center for Folklife, such standards and respect were followed. But in 1999, that was not the case for the temporary exhibit *Santo Pinholé: A Saint for Photography* at the National Museum of American History.

Elizabeth Kay, a New Mexico artist, decided to honor Ansel Adams through her creation of a retablo, a wooden-frame religious painting. She decided to use the New Mexico santo tradition, a practice that is almost five hundred years old, to honor Adams, even though Adams is not considered a saint within the Catholic Church or community. What Kay did is what scholars call cultural appropriation, the distorted use of other peoples' traditions or beliefs as one's own. That the Smithsonian decided to display her work was problematic, but that the curator did not indicate in the text that Kay's retablo was a spoof was doubly problematic because it left the viewer with the impression that Adams was considered a saint or that santeros, the artists that create santos, simply made up saints as part of their devotional art. The exhibit was troubling enough that the Latino Working Committee (LWC)—a group of Latinx staff, curators, and employees of the Smithsonian—called for a meeting with the curator to explain why the exhibit was produced, and why so poorly.

The *Santo Pinholé* exhibit's failure to provide any significant background information about the santo tradition, or that the exhibit was a spoof of a well-honored tradition, should not have been a surprise to the curator. During peer review, a process where scholars provide feedback and recommendations for an exhibit, the reviewers pointed out several issues, particularly the problem of cultural appropriation. However, the curator rejected the concerns and suggestions. It was a tense meeting that only resulted in the addition of text indicating that the exhibit was a spoof. The exhibit was not removed and was allowed to continue. Disappointment flooded the ranks of LWC members. We lost our battle for respect. It was a polite rejection based on supposed intellectual/scholarly grounds that outsiders can evaluate other peoples' cultures and history objectively, while the community should not be allowed to have a say in their representation because of a supposed lack of objectivity. The argument was bunk. The exhibit encapsulated the very point of the "Willful Neglect" report, which stated that Latinx scholarly voices are ignored.

~

The struggle to belong is found not only in the politics of the street, but in official institutions that are supposed to be inclusive of all Americans. Looking back on my time at the Smithsonian and how my family's stories and early life shaped me, I understand that for many Americans—including my own parents—being seen as American is a struggle that can be tiring and long. I felt that fatigue in 1999; I still feel it now. People like Olivia and Cynthia and others with the LWC continue to struggle within the Smithsonian, fighting for inclusive Latinx exhibits and programming. I was a small part of that struggle—and the fight for change—more than twenty years ago. I am a beneficiary of these struggles.

When I get down about our continued struggles to be seen as American, what revives me is striking a match, hearing the crack of burning mesquite, smelling the smoke, and listening to Country Roland Band. As I season the meat, I remember the stories my family told me, knowing that I come from a long line of americanos, those born on both sides of the river.

So, yes, there are many of us Mexicans in Texas. I come from those who helped make America.

MORNING PEOPLE

by **DIANA LÓPEZ**

When it comes to "early bird or night owl," I'm a night owl—and not because I'm sneaking out to party with my friends or bingeing on Netflix or writing great American novels or whatever it is that night owls do. No, it's because of insomnia. I lie down and my mind races. It all-out sprints, fifty-yard dashes, one after another. They start with someone's stupid tweet. Maybe it's about climate change, how we shouldn't get worked up, which makes me think about turtles since there are too many females, their gender determined by the temperature of the sand—which then makes me wonder, if we were mostly women, how would babies get made—which leads me to clones and Dolly the sheep and then *Frankenstein*—which takes me to Halloween costumes, and to Halloween, how it's not the same as Día de los Muertos, even though the two get lumped together with people painting themselves like calaveras and partying and forgetting that it's a *holy* holiday, which gets me thinking about all the things that get whitewashed in America, which leads me to the border wall and people saying we need to keep the Mexicans out, which gives me all kinds of bad feelings because even though I'm not Mexican-Mexican, I *am* Mexican American. *Someone* in my past came over. Then again, as we say in South Texas, "We didn't cross the border; the border crossed us," which happened, specifically, after the Treaty of Guadalupe Hidalgo, so now I'm thinking about my history class, how I got a C, even though I studied very, very hard. On and on it goes, one mind-sprint after another, until finally, hours later, I'm asleep.

So waking up is a process, and step one is pushing the snooze button five or six times. It is *not* Papá Grande turning on the light and singing—*singing!*—"Zip-a-dee-doo-dah, zip-a-dee-ay. My, oh my, what a wonderful day."

I pull the blanket over my face. "What's so good about it?"

He's too happy to be offended. He just yanks the blanket and says, "Well, let's find out, mi criatura." He never calls me Leti, always some nickname like criatura or flaca or Tweety Bird.

I am *so* not a morning person and neither is Mom, yet here we are, trudging to my grandparents' Subaru Forester for an insanely long road trip all the way from Corpus Christi, Texas, to Yellowstone National Park.

I'll sleep in the car, I promise myself, but I can't get comfy. First, the car's stuffed with luggage and camping gear. An ice chest is crammed between Mom and me, and she keeps nudging it over, making the buckle of the seat belt dig into my hip. I've got a pillow, but every position gives me a crick in the neck.

Meanwhile, my grandparents slurp their coffee and crunch their granola bars and crinkle all those wrappers.

"I can't sleep!" I complain.

Mom opens her eyes but shuts them again. She's pretending.

"Why do you want to sleep through such a beautiful morning?" Papá Grande says. Then, to my grandma, "Remember, mi amor, when the trucks used to take us to Robstown for the cotton?"

Mamá Grande peeks back at me. "Did we ever tell you how we fell in love?"

"Yes! Like a million times!" They make the cotton fields sound like enchanted forests, when all the migrant stories I've ever heard have people stooped over, sweating, and living in pigsties. I wonder, "Hey, how did you guys go to the bathroom when you were out there?"

"It was easier for the men," Mamá Grande says.

"The point is," Papá Grande goes on, "we wouldn't have met if we were sleepyheads. Isn't that right, mi amor?" Instead of answering, my grandma leans over and kisses him.

Mom's silent through all of this. She's still pretending to sleep. She pretends all the way through San Antonio and Austin, finally opening her eyes when we're at Georgetown, but even then, not engaging. At the rest stop, she gets down to pee like the rest of us, but other than that, she's a zombie, and all because Dad dumped her. She can't get over how he dumped her.

Finally we're in Dallas to pick up the rest of our family. I haven't seen them in a couple of years. Mom and Aunt Ceci are eleven months apart, but they aren't close, probably since they live in different cities. Uncle Paul is just Uncle Paul, a man of few words.

My primo Fonzie is a year older than me. His real name is Alfonso, but Papá Grande started calling him Fonzie when he was little and the name stuck. It's from a TV show called *Happy Days*. "Fonzie would snap his fingers," Mamá Grande once told me, "and I'd swoon." But *our* Fonzie isn't swoon-worthy. He's a dweeb, always defining words and uttering random facts. When he talks, it's like someone reading Wikipedia.

The last time I saw him, he was a toothpick with zits, but that isn't who exits my primo's house. Some *other* guy walks out. He kinda looks like Fonzie, but he isn't a dweeb. He's all muscled. He's got scars on his cheeks, but they don't look bad. And his hair, it's longish and dark; his eyes, a light caramel.

A sigh escapes me. Is this what swooning feels like? I should slap myself. I'm not supposed to swoon for a primo.

"Hey, Leti," he says, punching my shoulder like I'm on his baseball team.

"Hey, Fonzie." I'm supposed to hug him, right? I try, but I'm clumsy and self-conscious. I give him an awkward pat on the back instead.

Then I go to my aunt and uncle once Mom finishes hugging them. No clumsy moves there. My uncle's telling her, "Sorry to hear about you and Mike," and my aunt's saying, "Yes, mi hermanita, we're so, so sorry, but just because he left, you shouldn't let yourself go like this," and my mom, my poor mom, she doesn't bother to straighten her very wrinkled T-shirt or run fingers through her very tangled hair.

"Well, what are you gonna do?" she says. She's not exactly talking to us. She's thinking aloud.

Maybe this trip was a mistake. She didn't want to come, but we insisted. *I* insisted because she's been moping around since Dad left. I moped around too, but it's been six months now. I'm not letting him ruin another day. So when my grandparents suggested a vacation and she said no, I said, "Maybe some fresh air," and "Maybe a change of scenery." She agreed, finally, obviously, but here she is, still moping. Then again, we're in the Dallas suburbs. We haven't exactly hit fresh air or a change of scenery yet.

"¡Vámanos!" Papá Grande says, urging us to the cars. Aunt Ceci, Uncle Paul, and Fonzie get into their black Suburban, stuffed with camping gear just like our SUV.

Then it's two more days of driving. There's not much to say about Oklahoma, Kansas, and the eastern part of Colorado. We eat soggy bologna sandwiches and Doritos, and when I complain, I get a lecture from Mamá and Papá Grande about how they never had vacations or a car or anything as fancy as a bologna sandwich.

"We ate beans. Always beans. And if we were lucky, on a corn tortilla."

I try talking to Fonzie, since he's my age, but he's always with his earbuds. I wonder about his playlist. Who's on it? Does it have a theme? At one of the rest stops, I tug his sleeve. "What's on your playlist?" I ask.

"Audiobooks and podcasts," he says.

What kind of dude listens to audiobooks and podcasts? I can't even imagine it.

The landscape gets more interesting once we pass Denver, but it doesn't make the *trip* more interesting. I've got *A Lesson Before Dying* with me since it's on my summer reading list, but reading in the car gives me motion sickness, so I'm stuck staring out the window. I can't even text my friends since there's no reception out here. Then, finally, we get to Yellowstone, and yes, it's freaking beautiful.

We enter the park, and there are elk, bison, and so many birds. I have no words; only words born here—native to this land and the people who once lived here—could describe how beautiful it is. English doesn't cut it. Maybe Spanish does, but all I know are nouns—tierra, árbol, cielo. I blame my parents. Their style of teaching was pointing at things and asking me to repeat—mesa, piso, ventana—but they never actually *spoke* to me in Spanish, never challenged me with sentences. No one ever did. That's the power of American English. It pushes other languages aside, and now we'll never know the words for this beauty.

It's late afternoon when we reach the campsite. The men get to work, setting up tents. Fonzie grabs the one for Mom and me. He inspects the ground. "You like this spot?" he asks, pointing. I shrug, but Mom says, "It's a good spot, mijo."

He gets down on his knees, unfolds our tent, and the way he's doing it makes me think of someone turning down a bed. Then he grabs the stakes, and . . . I don't know . . . they're like phallic symbols. He pounds them into the ground, the mallet going up and down, like people having sex. He gets it assembled in about ten minutes. He's so efficient and . . . and . . . *manly*. Then he unzips the little door, and that zipping sound makes me look at his fly.

I'm such a pervert suddenly. But I can't help it! My primo . . . out here in the wild . . . he looks good.

But he *shouldn't* because we're related. What's wrong with me? I need serious help! I shake my head and blink a few times, trying to correct my perspective.

For dinner, hot dogs, and they're delicious. Then Fonzie says, "Let's go to the ranger talk." He's already grabbing a flashlight. I follow him, and so do my grandparents and uncle. Mom and Aunt Ceci stay behind.

The ranger talk is in a small amphitheater. It's already crowded, so Fonzie and I let the viejitos find spots on the benches while we sit on the ground. Some girls are nearby. They keep glancing over, and Fonzie glances *their* way and gives a little nod. They giggle. He winks. I scoot closer to him, saying I'm cold. He offers his jacket, and when I put it on, it still has his warmth and his scent. I look at the girls again. They turn away.

Good.

The talk is about wolves, how they're a "keystone species." They used to be here but got killed off. Then there were too many elk and too many coyotes, which meant fewer trees, gophers, and birds. Then, in 1995, wolves were captured in Canada and reintroduced to the park, and now the land is healing.

"Any questions?" the ranger asks.

Fonzie raises his hand. "Were you here when '06 was around?"

"Yes, I was," the ranger says. "Saw her with my own eyes. She was glorious." He talks on, answering other people's questions.

"Who's '06?" I whisper to Fonzie.

"Come on. You seriously don't know?" It's like I've asked for the location of the sky. "She's the most famous wolf in the world."

"Really? There's such a thing as celebrity wolves?"

He doesn't reply because he's focused on the ranger again, who's saying, "The best place to spot them is Lamar Valley, but it's a couple of hours from here. You'd have to leave early. They're most active in the morning."

After the ranger talk we head back, but it isn't a peaceful night because we hear Mom's and Aunt Ceci's raised voices even before we reach the campsite. My aunt's saying, "I'm not surprised. Saw this coming a long time ago." And Mom's saying, "Quit acting like you're better than me." And Aunt Ceci's saying, "It's not an act, hermana." And that's when I *think* Mom says, "You bitch." But no. She couldn't have. She probably called my aunt a witch or a snitch or some other *-itch*y word.

We rush toward the campsite, and when we get there, Mamá Grande gets between them. "Ya! Ya!" she says. "What's all this noise?"

They don't answer. After a minute, Aunt Ceci stomps toward the restroom, Uncle Paul following. Meanwhile, Mom ducks into the tent without a word.

"Why are they mad at each other?" I ask.

Mamá Grande shrugs, though she probably knows the answer.

Fonzie doesn't seem to care. He's more interested in the wolves. "So what time should we head to Lamar Valley? You think four thirty?"

"That sounds good," Papá Grande says.

Are they kidding? They want to leave at four thirty in the morning? To see wolves?

I've had enough of my crazy family. I enter the tent and snuggle into my sleeping bag. Mom's probably awake, but she's upset and not talking. I try to keep still, but there's a rock at my shoulder and it's under the tent, so I can't just push it aside. I shift around. Now there's another rock, this one poking my back. I shift again and again, three or four more times until I find a rock-free position. Then the mind-sprints. First about my primo. I still have his jacket and it smells so good. Then about the wolves, and this celebrity wolf that has the ranger and my primo all excited. And what was up with those girls? Were they seriously trying to flirt with my cousin? Sure, he's hot, but beneath all that hotness is a nerd.

I listen to my mom's soft breath, and layers upon layers of insects, and scuffling from a bison, maybe, or a bear. What if a bear's out there? What if it tears open the tent? I don't even have a pocketknife to defend myself. How can anyone sleep in a place like this? I need to sleep! I'm tired. It's been a long day, and it'll be a longer day tomorrow.

Leti, go to sleep. Stop thinking!

Ordering myself around doesn't work, so I try counting sheep, visualizing fluffy puffs leaping over a fence. One sheep, two sheep, three. Wait a minute! What's that? A wolf again!

This one in sheep's clothing! How does my primo know so much about wolves, anyway? And why does he want to wake up at some ungodly hour to see them?

Seems like Papá Grande zips open our door and says "Rise and shine" before I ever drift off.

"Leti and I are staying," Mom says. "You can tell us about it when you get back."

My eyes are closed, but I can hear him. He takes a full minute before he zips up the door and walks away.

"Thanks, Mom," I whisper. She reaches over, gives my shoulder an affectionate squeeze, and finally . . . finally . . . I sleep.

When I wake up, Mom's at the picnic table, organizing things. I'm glad we're alone, because she understands that, for me, waking up is a process, never mind the inconvenience of camping—a trek to the restroom and the line once I'm there, the counter full of water and dabs of other people's toothpaste. I'm missing the city, the luxury of a real bed and a restroom that doesn't require a hike, but when I step back outside, there's a raven. He tilts his head to look at me. Then he seems to speak.

Look around, he says. *Take a deep breath.*

When I do, I see trees and mountains and sky. I sniff at the air. And suddenly I can't explain it, but out here, the scent of time is in the rocks and dirt. It reminds me that the universe is old and vast, while I am young and tiny. Maybe I should be sad about being so insignificant, but if I'm not important, then neither are my problems or the problems of this world, and that gives me something to smile about.

"Thanks, Raven," I say, and I swear he nods.

I'm in a better mood when I return to camp. Mom's at the propane stove, mixing Spam with eggs. We eat, and finally I ask what I've been wondering about since we got back to the campsite. "Why were you and Aunt Ceci fighting last night?"

"It's nothing," Mom answers. "Don't worry. Your aunt just gets on my nerves. You know how she is. Always acting like she's better than me."

It's true. My aunt—how do they say?—se cree mucho.

"Why is she like that?" I ask.

"I don't know. She's always been jealous."

She doesn't seem jealous to me, just stuck-up and always gloating.

"You know what?" Mom says. "This place is beautiful, and I'm not letting anyone ruin this trip."

We don't have a chance to say more because the Suburban pulls up. Mom and I have just finished breakfast, but it's really lunchtime. She points at the skillet. She's made enough for everyone, so they grab tortillas to make Spam-and-egg taquitos.

"Sleepyheads," Papá Grande says, "you missed the wolves."

"Did you get pictures?" I ask.

Fonzie hands me his phone. "Dozens!"

I scan the pics. All I see is a field.

"You have to zoom in," Fonzie explains.

I zoom.

"See those grayish dots?" He's pointing. "That's them."

I squint, trying to make out the shapes, but they look like wisps of lint to me.

Fonzie takes back his phone. "I wish I had a *real* camera."

"But we got a good look with the binoculars, eh?" Papá Grande still has them around his neck.

"Seeing wolves is one of the highlights of visiting Yellowstone," Aunt Ceci says, sounding like a travel brochure. "Too bad you missed it, but I guess you needed some beauty sleep."

She's looking at me, but she's really talking to Mom, who makes a big show of rolling her eyes. I can tell Aunt Ceci wants to sass back, but before she can say anything, Fonzie starts rambling about Yellowstone being the first national park of the United States.

It's a long history lesson. He's still talking while we drive to Dragon's Mouth Spring, a place where mud boils. The whole place stinks like rotten eggs, but I get used to it. I'm actually fascinated by the boiling mud, the way it gurgles and pops.

～～～

On the way back to camp later, we stop at a valley to take pictures of bison, all the while listening to Fonzie explain the difference between bison and buffalo, coyotes and wolves, elk and moose. He moves from one topic to another. No breaks. The entire day, his voice, but I don't mind. I'm actually impressed.

"How do you know all this stuff?" I ask.

Aunt Ceci answers. "He's taking all AP classes. He's already at the college level. Tell her your SAT scores, mijo."

He's suddenly shy. "No, Mom."

"Tell her."

"No. Leave it alone. It's not a big deal."

"Well," Aunt Ceci insists, "let's just say he can go to whatever college he wants."

Again, she's looking at me, but she's *really* talking to Mom, and what she's saying is *My child is smarter than your child because I'm smarter than you.*

I know Mom understands the *real* message, but she just shrugs. Good. She's not letting Aunt Ceci win.

~

The next day, we go to Old Faithful, a geyser named for the fact that it shoots steaming water over a hundred feet into the air every ninety-two minutes. At least, that's what Fonzie says. We find a good viewing spot and wait. It'll still be a while, but soon the place is crowded with people speaking dozens of languages. Mamá and Papá Grande always mix a little Spanish with their English, but for some reason, they're speaking only Spanish now.

"What's up with them?" I ask my mom.

"I guess they want to seem international," she says.

I get it. Sometimes it's embarrassing to be American, to be *Mexican* American, when so many potential compadres are stuck in border detention centers. This country . . . does it love or hate me . . . love or hate my kind? I'm always wondering.

Suddenly everyone aims their cameras and phones at the mound before us. It's bubbling over. Then nothing. We keep waiting. The suspense! Then it bubbles up again, and there's a big spurt, followed by a *bigger* spurt, followed by a gushing stream of water, shooting into the sky. The magnitude! There's this collective "Wow!" and I realize—the sound of amazement is the same in every language.

Here I am—with my family, but also with strangers, some from other countries, who carry other beliefs. In the past, maybe even right now, we've been at war with these people, but here, our governments don't matter. All we care about is watching this enormous spout of water. Every ninety-two minutes, Old Faithful brings people together. We should gather the world leaders to see it. Maybe they'd stop fighting. How could anyone fight in front of something as beautiful as this?

The geyser finally settles down, and the crowd thins out, everyone going in different directions. My grandparents' Spanish has paid off because they've met a couple from Colombia and decide to join them at the Old Faithful Lodge Cafeteria for lunch.

The rest of us go on a hike, but only fifteen minutes in, Aunt Ceci's complaining.

"Let's go back," she tells us.

"No," Mom says. "You can go if you want, but we're gonna keep walking."

"But there's nothing to see."

"There's this Anemone Geyser," Mom says, reading the sign in front of a formation that really does look like a sea anemone.

"So what?" Aunt Ceci says. "We've already seen the main attraction."

Mom ignores her, moves along.

Aunt Ceci huffs, then shifts to my uncle. "How about it, Paul?"

"I think I'll keep walking too," he says, following Mom.

Fonzie and I just stand there, watching this exchange.

"You are *not* going with her," Aunt Ceci says. She marches to Uncle Paul, grabs his arm, and forcefully stops him.

"Whoa, Mom!" Fonzie says.

My mom laughs. "You think I'm going to steal your husband?" That about does it.

Aunt Ceci, *not* laughing, says, "You couldn't steal him if you tried!"

And now they're going back and forth, verbally jabbing each other. Uncle Paul gets between them, holds them back because it looks like they want to throw punches. Meanwhile, Fonzie and I are going, "Mom! Mom!" trying to calm them down. People are stopping to look. It's embarrassing, this telenovela right here at Yellowstone National Park.

"Enough!" Uncle Paul says. "Let's go," he tells Aunt Ceci. And there he is, fast-walking back to the trailhead, Aunt Ceci jogging to catch up.

When they're out of earshot, I confront my mom. "What is going on?"

Mom glances at Fonzie. She clearly doesn't want to talk in front of him, but I have to know.

"Why are you talking about stealing Uncle Paul?" I ask.

"I'm just joking around," Mom answers. "She's so serious all the time." She faces us, grabs our hands. "Sorry your parents are acting like children. But look. We're in a beautiful place. Let's just enjoy ourselves."

Fonzie and I glance at each other. He has questions too, I can tell, but we decide not to push it. We follow Mom's suggestion and try our best to forget about the fight. It's awkward at first, but soon we're stopping at every geyser and pool, reading every poster, and taking pictures.

After a while, Mom finds a bench and urges us to keep walking while she rests. She closes her eyes and lifts her face to the sun. I can tell she wants some private time.

Fonzie and I leave her there, go off by ourselves.

"Is she okay?" Fonzie asks.

"Yeah," I say.

So now we're alone, and we walk quietly for a few moments. But soon he's giving me a lecture about how this is a caldera, how there have been three massive volcanic eruptions in Yellowstone's history, the last one over six hundred thousand years ago. We're basically in the giant bowl that's left behind. He must have researched before coming. I guess I could've researched too, but it's a lot more interesting to hear about places when I'm actually there. This is the first time I've encountered the word *caldera*, but not from a book. I'm actually *standing* in one.

Later that afternoon, we go to the Grand Prismatic Spring, a pool like a rainbow because it's blue in the middle, then green, then yellow, then red. There's a boardwalk, and as we walk along, Fonzie explains that the reddish arms of the spring are bacterial mats, that we're actually walking on a giant petri dish. Then he talks about primordial soup, how all life began from these microbial hot spots.

Two years ago—two *weeks* ago—all this lecturing would have annoyed me no end. I didn't come here to learn anything. Just wanted to take pictures and forget about my dad. But I'm surprisingly interested in what Fonzie's saying. I'm listening to his words *and* to his voice. It's deeper now. I want to put a finger on his neck to feel the vibrations there. And, yes, I know he's my cousin, that I shouldn't feel this way. I'm sure God's reading my impure thoughts, but I'm more embarrassed than afraid.

~

The next day we go to Mammoth Hot Springs, but it's not until the last day, when we go to the Grand Canyon of Yellowstone, that I finally learn—and see—the yellow stones for which the park is named. Fonzie explains that they're rhyolite, a fancy word for hardened lava.

The whole time, Mom and Aunt Ceci keep their distance. I still don't know what their fight was about, but I don't ask. And I can't help but notice that in spite of everything, the change of scenery and fresh air is working miracles on Mom. She's talking more, making jokes like she used to before Dad left. We've been eating takeout or frozen dinners for the past few months, but here she's cooking again, and *enjoying* it. Aunt Ceci still annoys Mom with all her comparisons and bragging, but out here Mom's fighting back. She doesn't look defeated. She seems almost back to her old self, or maybe even a *better* self.

~

Finally it's the last night of our trip. We've got three days of driving ahead; then we'll be in the city again, back to internet access and all those reminders that things aren't right in the world—stupid tweets from our celebrities and politicians, the latest shooting at some church or bar or Walmart, the detention centers along the border, and the drug wars, trade wars, and *war* wars. My screwed-up life in the house where my father no longer lives.

But all of that can wait. For now I enjoy the moment.

"It's almost time for the ranger talk," Fonzie says. The rest of the family decides to stay behind and pack so we can leave first thing in the morning.

"You gatitos go along," Papá Grande says.

So Fonzie and I head to the amphitheater, but I don't really want to go.

"Maybe we can skip the talk tonight," I suggest. "Maybe we can find a good place to see the stars."

Fonzie doesn't argue, just looks around. We spot a picnic table in a clearing. We climb on it and lie back to see the sky.

"So that's the Milky Way?" I ask, pointing. Instead of a ranger talk, I get another Fonzie talk. He can't resist telling me about the galaxy, how every star is a sun and how we're looking at the past because it takes so long for the light to reach us. It's interesting. It really is, but I'm going "shush," and then more softly, "shush," and then, whispering, "Let's just look." And we do. For the longest time. The stars seem to press against me, and I inhale, remembering the raven and the scent of time in the rocks and dirt, and I listen—to the breeze and the scuffling that no longer frightens me, and, out of nowhere, to Fonzie's voice. Only, this time he isn't lecturing, just saying my name.

"Leti?"

"Yeah?"

He doesn't answer. I can feel him thinking, deciding. Then he leans over, his face above mine. If he moves an inch closer, he'll be in range for a kiss, but he's waiting, as if asking for permission. I know kissing him would be so, *so* wrong. Then again, ever since we picked him up in Dallas, I've been wishing he *weren't* my cousin but some boy I met at school. Why can't he be a boy I met at school? He doesn't move, and I don't move, and we stay caught in this moment of indecision. I wish I could make it last—how we are both wanting and *not* wanting to act—but he turns his head suddenly. "Hear that?" he asks. Then there's a light on us and familiar voices—*Oh shit*—it's our family.

Please, Earth, crack open and swallow me now.

I never thought you could gasp for more than a second, but Aunt Ceci manages. Meanwhile, my grandparents are upon us, Mamá Grande grabbing me by the arm, and Papá Grande grabbing Fonzie by the ear.

"Ow, ow!" Fonzie cries.

When Aunt Ceci finds her voice, she says, "What's wrong with you two? You're primos. This is incest. Incest! Your babies will have webbed fingers and thirteen toes!"

"We didn't do anything!" Fonzie says.

"Not yet," Aunt Ceci counters.

"Not ever!" he says, and I echo, "Never!" realizing at this moment that I'm speaking the truth. I was never going to kiss Fonzie, no matter how much I wanted to.

Everyone's scandalized, except for Mom. She thinks it's funny.

"All this drama." She laughs.

And now Aunt Ceci's in her face. "Is that what you call it?"

Mom's still laughing, but with this showdown, she doesn't laugh for long. She leans forward, nose-to-nose with my aunt, and here we are again, witness to another fight. My grandparents and uncle are already getting between them.

Aunt Ceci points at me. "She's trouble. My mijo. He's a good boy. He doesn't lie. If he says he's going to a ranger talk, then that's where he's going. She probably—"

"¡Cállate!" Papá Grande says, and Uncle Paul scolds, "Cecilia!"

But Aunt Ceci will *not* give up. "The apple doesn't fall far from the tree. I knew she'd be trouble someday, just like her father."

That's it. "What is she talking about, Mom?" Now I *must* know.

"Nothing."

But Aunt Ceci explains. "Your father left your mother for another woman."

The breath goes out of me. "Is that true?" But I don't really need to ask. I suspected it, have *been* suspecting it, ever since Dad started going to the gym at all hours but never lost weight or got fit. My eyes start to water, and just as quickly, Mom puts an arm around my shoulders.

"What goes around comes around," Aunt Ceci adds.

"What does that *even* mean?" I cry, but as I say it, I start to understand. "Wait a minute." I look at my aunt. "Was my dad *your* boyfriend first?"

She nods. "Till your mother stole him."

"I didn't steal him!" Mom shouts. "You drove him away."

"Well, I guess *you're* the one who drove him away *this* time."

"That's enough!" Uncle Paul says finally. He's looking at Aunt Ceci. "This happened twenty years ago, and you're still angry? How do you think *I* feel every time you bring it up?"

He doesn't let her answer because he's stomping off, followed by Fonzie and then my grandparents. Mom and Aunt Ceci watch them leave. I hope they realize how stupid they are for fighting about this, for hurting each other, for hurting Uncle Paul and me. I feel like such a fool, thinking I'd found a pocket of peace on this warring planet.

"Thanks a lot!" I say to them. "This was freaking delightful!"

And now *I* walk off. No. I *run*. I pass everyone on my way to camp, and when I get there, I duck into the tent and then the sleeping bag, even though I really have to pee. But who cares? I won't sleep anyway. Not with these rocks stabbing my shoulders and this anger stabbing my heart.

My mom comes in then. "Leti?" she says softly. But I turn away.

~

It's still dark when Papá Grande wakes us the next morning. This time I don't complain. I don't say anything at all because I'm still too mad to speak. My uncle and my grandpa have pointed their headlights at the camp so we can finish packing. Mom and Aunt Ceci are ignoring each other, and everyone's keeping Fonzie and me apart. We can't even *look* at each other without a warning glance from someone—mostly from Mamá Grande.

Then we head out, but we don't leave the park just yet. We head to the Lake Yellowstone Hotel, which is by a lake. Papá Grande stops at a SCENIC OVERLOOK sign and a deck that faces east.

"I want to watch the sunrise," he explains.

We line up at the rail, the water softly lapping beneath us. It's cold and dark, but we wait.

"Did we ever tell you how we fell in love?"

I groan, but Mamá Grande begins, and I hear the whole story again—how the trucks picked them up, how they watched the sunrise on their way to Robstown, how beautiful it was when it gave its gold light to the fields. Again, no mention of the heat and bugs and blisters, of the reason they were picking cotton in the first place, because they were hungry and poor and of a time when Mexicans had few options. None of that. According to my grandparents, the cotton fields were as beautiful as any scenic spot along the roads of Yellowstone National Park, and when they tell the story, even though I know the harsh truths behind it, I imagine them working and falling in love while dancing in the clouds.

"Mira," Papá Grande says, pointing at the horizon. "The first finger of the sun. See how it reaches for us?"

He puts his arm around Mamá Grande, and she leans into him. We watch the sun lighting the sky, one finger at a time, like a fist unfurling.

"Paul?" Aunt Ceci says.

"Shush," he answers, kissing her.

Then my aunt again: "Hermanita?" She's reaching for my mother. Uncle Paul and my grandparents are between them, but Mom stretches out her arm and takes her sister's hand. Fonzie and I are on opposite sides of all this, but I lean forward and catch his eye. He smiles back at me. We will probably never be alone again. We'll move on, but I will always remember our last night in Yellowstone and that moment of sweet suspense.

Mi familia. We watch this sunrise in a land so far away from our homes in Texas. I guess we're morning people after all.

ODE TO MY PAPI

by GUADALUPE GARCÍA MCCALL

In loving memory of my papi, el Señor Onésimo García
(1940–2020)—

because you did so much to make us strong.

> He could only give me one dollar
> a week. On Fridays, when I'd serve him
> dinner after work, he'd pull the single dollar bill
> out of his worn wallet with weathered
> hands—hands that had cut and transformed
> mesquite, planks, shingles, tiles, and cement.
>
> In cold, sleet, rain, and sun, my papi's
> weathered hands framed offices, erected hotels,
> covered roofs, threw cement, built homes,
> and helped put up a dam named Amistad
> in Fort Worth, Galveston, Eagle Pass, Del Rio, and

every other town along the Rio Grande and beyond.

That dollar, he knew, would buy me
a billion galaxies, countless stars, oceans,
a rain forest, and miles and miles of desert—fictions,
dark and light, sweet and tart, all of them
affordable, within his means, pulled out
of the ten-cent bin at our local library.

Those books transported me. Since then,
I've traveled a long road, negotiated borders,
been recognized and awarded
gold medallions, plaques, and certificates
because those strong hands provided,
nurtured, made me feel loved, adored.

In giving me what little he could,
my papi gave me the universe.

THE BODY BY THE CANAL

by **DAVID BOWLES**

September of 1987 wasn't much different from September of 1986. My dad was still gone, we were still living on food stamps and welfare, I was still the lone freak at my high school, trapped in this conservative border town, unusual even for the circle of outcasts that had formed around me. Every girl I dated dumped me. The teachers thought I was too smug for my own good. I crossed out the days on my calendar, counting down toward graduation. Escape.

Then the neighbors moved in downstairs, and everything changed.

It was a Saturday. Luis, Javi, and I were across the street at the Pharr Civic Center, taking turns falling off a beat-up skateboard we'd scammed off a rich white kid from McAllen.

"Is that a dude or a chick?" Luis asked.

I looked over at the thin, elegant figure struggling to pull a box from the trunk of an old sedan. Longish hair teased wildly. Knee-high boots with one-inch heels. Bangles, bracelets, and a bright pink Swatch on the left wrist. A satiny black shirt with a frilly collar. Lips bright with color. Eyelids shaded.

As out of place in this shitty neighborhood as a peacock among chickens. I knew the feeling.

"I dunno," I said. But my stomach did a pirouette as the newcomer turned to look at us.

Boy or girl, the kid was beautiful.

And from my own experience, this town would do all it could to destroy that beauty.

"Only one way to find out," Javi said, stamping on the back of the skateboard so it popped straight up. Snatching it from the air, he gestured with his chin. "Let's go say hello."

I was strangely conscious of my own appearance as we walked back across Kelly Avenue to the Section 8 apartments where I lived with my mom and little brother, Fernando. Torn Levi 501s. Turquoise canvas high-tops, off-brand. A random white T-shirt with purple blotches that had seemed gnarly when I bought it but now made me feel like a total poseur. Since it was Saturday, I hadn't bothered to curl the bangs of my bi-level hairdo, which reached my shoulders in back.

I figured I looked a mess. Still, I got out in front of Javi and Luis, anyway. They were a little ranchero, always putting their feet in their mouths when meeting cool people, even though they meant well.

"Hey," I said, waving as we approached. "Need any help?"

"Nah," the newbie said, and I could tell he was a guy though his voice was soft. The homophobes at our school were going to have a field day. "I've got it. Thanks."

"My name's Oscar, by the way," I added. "I live right above you, in two eleven. These are my friends Luis and Javi. They live . . . elsewhere."

I waved my hand vaguely, and he smiled. Glints of amber in his eyes caught the morning sun, sparkling like gold. My palms began to ache.

"Ariel," he said, pronouncing it in Spanish: ah-RYEL. "Ariel Ortega."

A glance told me that the box he was balancing on the bumper was full of records.

"Cool look," said Luis, who sported a crew cut because of JROTC. "Like a little punk, a little hair metal . . ."

"It's gothic," I said, and Ariel's honey eyes widened. "A bit more Siouxsie Sioux than Ian Curtis, but still."

Ariel tilted his head, and something fluttered in my chest. "Try Robert Smith. What was your name again?"

"Oscar," I said. "Oscar Garza."

There was a strange pause. Somewhere a whip-poor-will gave its plaintive cry. There was a skull ring on Ariel's right hand, I noticed. His fingers were slender and manicured.

"Welcome to Pharr, Texas, bro," Luis said. "We're sort of the outsiders at the high school, so, yeah. You'll wind up with us eventually."

"Pardon me?" Ariel asked.

Javi gestured at the newcomer's clothes. "Let's just say you're not the typical student."

"But that's okay," I interjected, narrowing my eyes at my friends pointedly. "It's a backwoods rancho, but it's survivable. Just make sure the counselors put you in college prep classes with me."

"With us," Javi corrected. I heard him sigh, though I didn't look away from Ariel. Couldn't. There was a jingle as Javi fished his keys from his pocket. "Come on, Luis. I've got an afternoon shift at Starlite Burger. I'll drop you at your uncle's place on the way."

"Wait, what about . . ." Luis began, but Javi had already walked over to el Moco, his dad's green Impala. Luis glanced at Ariel and me. He took a knowing breath and nodded. "Órale, I'm coming. Nice meeting you, Ariel."

〜

I ended up helping Ariel set up his stereo after his mom, Gloria, found us talking music outside and invited me to lunch. She was pretty open about their situation: They'd been living in Austin, but Mr. Ortega was a drunken son of a bitch who wouldn't leave her precious boy alone. Rather than returning to California, where her family lived, she was trying to throw her abusive husband off the scent by coming to the Rio Grande Valley.

I had seen a couple of Cure videos on MTV, but I'd never listened to a full album, so Ariel lowered the needle on their latest: *Kiss Me, Kiss Me, Kiss Me.*

"When they toured with Siouxsie and the Banshees," Ariel explained, "Smith ended up taking over as guitarist for the other band. Being a Banshee changed him, I think. If you listen to their earlier music, it's kind of fake. Like he didn't know who he was. She opened his eyes. And now just listen, Oscar. Just listen."

I did. It was otherworldly, beautiful, haunting.

Smith started singing "Why Can't I Be You?" and Ariel, who had been sitting cross-legged on the floor, couldn't contain himself anymore. He leapt up and started to dance, his limbs lithe and balletic even amid all the frenzied post-punk moves.

I watched him, spellbound. His eyes caught mine, and he laughed, pulling me to my feet against my will.

I was a rocker. We don't dance.

But I did. I danced with absolute abandon, laughing at the joy of it.

We fell back on his bed, breathless, as slower songs followed. He talked to me about the lyrics, about the band's journey, the other groups I'd never heard of whose influences he swore he could distinguish.

"I play the guitar," I said out of the blue. "Javi, Luis, and me, we're trying to start a band."

Ariel propped his head on his palm as he turned to look at me. "What kind of music?"

I tried not to notice the feel of his breath on my arm.

"Don't know yet. Rock, definitely. Metal, we've been thinking. But this . . ."

He laid his other hand on my arm.

"I know! I'm going to record you a mixtape, Oscar. Only the very best from my carefully curated collection. I am *certain* you'll find inspiration."

"Órale," I said. "And I'll show you the ropes at PSJA High

School. I, uh, used to get bullied a lot, but I've figured out how to navigate the bola de rancheros there."

"We'll be each other's guides, then," he said, and there was something in his voice that made my pulse quicken.

~~~~~

As I had imagined, the usual suspects had all kinds of nicknames for Ariel. None were quite as creative as güero cacahuatero and mariposón, as I had been dubbed by the wannabe gangsters on campus. But I took Ariel to our counselor, Ms. Simpson, and helped him get the same schedule as Javi and me. Since he lived in government housing like I did, we rode the same bus, listening to music on his Walkman.

For a few weeks, life in those shitty apartments was actually a delight. Mom still worked her two jobs, Fernando still spent all his time across the breezeway with Speedy Espericueta, playing Super Mario Bros. on Speedy's NES. But instead of stewing in my room alone, reading the bleak German and Russian novels that had been keeping me company in the depths of my depression, I now had a fellow freak to help while the hours away. Unabashedly, I spent time every after-noon with my new friend.

When I wasn't hanging out with Ariel, listening to his amazing collection of LPs and reading the darker of the DC comics, I was up in my apartment, learning to play post-punk songs on my battered knockoff Fender. Javi and Luis still came to visit on the weekends, but the dynamic had changed. I could see that Ariel's presence disconcerted them.

"Is there anything you want to tell us, dude?" Javi asked one night when we got on the phone together using two-way calling.

"About?"

Luis cleared his throat. "You and Ariel, Oscar. Feels weird, the way you keep shutting us out. We figure . . . maybe you like him. As, uh, more than a friend."

"What?" I said, getting indignant to cover the panic welling up in my chest. How could they see through me like this? Was I that obvious to everyone? "Y'all never change. Always with your snide little comments about my clothes and hair."

"No, Oscar," Javi broke in. "That's not it. Yeah, we've teased you, but if you really like him, that's cool with us, carnal."

"Whatever. Pinches rancheros. You just can't handle a cool gothic kid from California."

They hung up on me. I deserved it, I guess. But I couldn't be honest with them. Better to pretend our little clique was being broken up by Ariel.

I wasn't about to exclude him.

I was growing to need him.

~~~

After Ariel's third week in Pharr, I grabbed my guitar and my sputtering amp and headed downstairs. As if he could sense me at the door, he opened before I knocked.

"¿Y esto?" he asked. "Are you planning to serenade me, Oscar Garza?"

I could feel my pale skin blushing beet red. "I just wanted to show you," I said. "I learned it."

"What?"

Before I could stop myself, I blurted, "Our song."

Pausing only briefly, he gave me a sweet smile.

"Come in, then. This calls for something special."

I went into his room and plugged in my guitar, sitting on the edge of his bed. He pulled the curtains closed and snapped a steel lighter open. I'd of course noticed the candles on his shelves before, but now he lit them, along with a stick of incense.

"Open your chakras, Oscar," he said, giving a soft laugh. "Let the music flow from the All."

Shaking my head and chuckling, I checked the tuning of my guitar and started to play. I'd slowed the tempo down and lowered the key to match my baritone better.

I couldn't bring myself to look him in the eye as I sang.

> *Everything you do is irresistible*
> *Everything you do is simply kissable*
> *Why can't I be you?*

I didn't even finish the song before Ariel stopped my hands on the strings, kneeling in front of me. His face was so close to mine, those lips that seemed to smile only for me, tears trembling in his eyes.

It had been months since my last kiss, back before Diana Alaniz had broken up with me.

And I had never kissed a boy before.

But I felt safe, safer than ever in my life.

I leaned forward and pressed my mouth to his. Sweet and warm, like mango just plucked from a tree.

We took our time, savoring that taste.

~~~

Over dinner that evening, my mother shared gossip from work.

"There's this drama teacher," she said. "From Mission or McAllen or somewhere. He's gone missing."

Fernando shrugged. "One less teacher in the world? I'm not gonna cry."

"Nando!" she scolded. "That's a terrible thing to say. But you're not letting me finish. They say he has the AIDS. That he's a homosexual and kept meeting his lovers even though he knew he could get them sick too."

I set my glass down, fuming in irritation. My mother was super religious. Ever since my uncle Samuel had come out of the closet back in 1980, she never missed an opportunity to mention how sinful his lifestyle was, how dangerous promiscuity could be, with AIDS and all the other "venereal diseases" that she liked to list like some sort of weird Rosary.

"Mom, we really don't want to hear this crap."

"Hey, some respect!" She glared at me. I already knew I reminded her of my deadbeat dad, the man she'd just divorced for abandonment. Every time I failed to live up to her expectations, she accused me of being just like him. "Anyway, they're saying that his lovers found out and came up with a plan to kidnap him."

Fernando looked at me, one eyebrow raised. "Mom watches too many telenovelas."

"I have no time for soap operas, Fernando Tomás Garza! I work myself to the bone long hours every day because your father ran off on us. So you boys just stay away from such sinful stuff, do you hear? Don't make me worry any more than I already do about you two being here alone."

I gave her a thumbs-up. "You bet, Mom. It's all copacetic."

It was her favorite word. Like a magic spell, it always calmed her down.

She crossed herself and kept eating.

~~~

After dinner, Ariel and I chatted on the phone for a while. He kept making vague references to our kiss. Part of me wanted to flirt too, but I couldn't stop thinking about the missing teacher. Couldn't get my mother's stupid voice out of my head. So I told Ariel the gossip.

"Of *course* it's a teacher," he grumbled. "Sleeping around like a slut. That's not what it's about, Oscar."

"No?" I said, though I had strong feelings about being faithful. I'd had several girlfriends since junior high and had never cheated on any of them.

"No. It's about following our hearts. When your heart is drawn to someone, how can you give it to another? Or your lips? Or your body?"

For a moment I imagined him, elegant and beautiful, unbuttoning his shirt . . .

"You're right. It's just a sore subject in my stupid family. My uncle's gay, and the rest of them, well, you know how Mexican men are about that shit."

There was silence on the other end. Then: "Yes, Oscar. I'm

very acquainted with it. My dad beat me enough times. I don't think I'll ever forget how Mexican men are toward folks like us."

Folks like us.

My stomach flip-flopped. What was I? What was I doing with this boy?

Why now? What was it about Ariel Ortega that made me risk discovery?

"Oscar? Say something."

"Ah, Ariel. I've, uh, I've got to hit the sack."

"There's no school tomorrow, sweet boy. It's a holiday. But okay. Get your rest. Maybe we can hang out in the afternoon, yeah?"

I swallowed heavily, my mind a jumble. "Yeah. Sure we can."

~~~

"There's a dead body by the canal."

I glanced up at Fernando. A couple of hours ago I had let him go across the breezeway to Speedy Espericueta's apartment, just to get him out of my hair. Since there was no school, I was stuck babysitting an eleven-year-old who relished getting himself in trouble.

Now here he was, sweaty and out of breath, feeding me a ridiculous line of crap.

"Nando, what the hell, man? I told you not to leave the complex. Mom'll kill me if she knows you went to the canal again."

"Did you hear me? There's a body there, Oscar. A dead one."

"Yeah, sure there is. Why don't you take a shower or something? You stink."

He shut the door and walked over to the sofa. I dog-eared my book and really looked at him. There was fear in his eyes, genuine horror like I hadn't seen him show since Dad left.

"Dude," Fernando said, his voice hoarse, quavering, "I'm not messing with you. We went down to go fishing, me and Speedy. Then we saw them—a guy's legs, sticking out of the weeds."

That final detail convinced me. Trying to stay calm, I grabbed the phone and dialed 911. I rattled off a summary of the situation, and the dispatcher said the Pharr PD would send someone by.

There was no way I was going to let the cops show up at this government housing complex, full of all sorts of marginalized people and criminals.

"I'm calling from a pay phone. We'll meet you at the canal," I said, hanging up.

Fernando looked at me, dumbfounded. "You don't have a car."

"Yeah, but Ariel's mother does. Come on."

"We shouldn't call Mom?" Fernando asked.

"No. Last thing she needs is more stress. Don't want her freaking out and leaving work. She'd probably call in sick at the other job too."

We need to get out of this place, I didn't say. *And for that we need every dime she can scrape together.*

My little brother just shrugged and went downstairs with me. I'd pretty much been his surrogate dad for the past four years, and though he preferred to act all independent, he tended to follow my lead.

A single knock was all it took. Ariel opened immediately.

"Can your mom drive us to the Ridge Road canal? My little brother thinks he saw a dead body. We're supposed to meet the police there."

Gloria Ortega was shocked, but she agreed. Fernando climbed into the passenger seat. Ariel and I got in the back.

As we drove away, I glanced at the block of Section 8 apartments, the last refuge of the disposed and discarded.

That's what we are, I thought as my eyes drifted over the motley assortment of clunkers in the pitted parking lot. *Discarded. Left behind.*

My heart was heavy. As if sensing my spiraling emotions, Ariel reached out and took my hand. I both wanted to lace my fingers with his and to pull away; I did neither. I just let him cradle my hand like a baby as Nando guided Gloria down to Ridge Road and up the dirt path that led to the canal.

"There it is!" my brother finally shouted. The old sedan bumped to a stop, and the four of us got out. The heat of the early autumn made everything hazy, bled color from the vegetation, leaving the meager brush pallid and dead. The hollow whine of cicadas drowned out all other noise—an ominous, predatory rattle. I wiped sweat from my face and followed Nando as he took a few hesitant steps away from the car. Behind me came Ariel and his mother, dead weeds crunching underfoot. For a moment my eyes were overwhelmed by the dusty brightness, but I squinted painfully as my little brother froze up.

And then I saw it.

Thrusting out dumbly onto the hard-packed gravel were two lifeless legs: pale, thin, coated with wiry black hair. One foot was covered by a black nylon sock; the other was bare, and I noticed with a strange sort of nausea that the man had not clipped his toenails in some time.

Gloria gasped, hurrying to pull Fernando back. Ariel came to a stop beside me, his shoulder touching mine.

Trembling, he gave whispered voice to my thoughts.

"It's him. The teacher."

A squad car pulled up. I could sense Gloria guiding my brother toward the officer who emerged, calling out to us. She must have spoken to him, but I couldn't be sure. As if from a great distance, I heard the officer call for an ambulance and backup. The dull hum of the cicadas filled my ears, thrummed in my skull like the low growl of some unseen machinery or massive beast.

I took another step. Ariel—arm around me, trying to hold me back, but I pulled away. I walked closer to the body until I could see more of him, nearly all of his torso. He was wearing black briefs and a white undershirt. Sickly weeds obscured his arms; his face was covered by the low, knotty branches of some thorny bush.

This is death. Abrupt. Meaningless. Dumb. A body, discarded, swallowed by the gaping jaws of the world. This is what they do to "folks like us," Ariel.

With a superhuman effort, I turned my back on the body.

Tears were streaming down Ariel's beautiful face. I wanted to hold him, wanted him to hold me, wanted to collapse into an embrace that would blot out the world so that only he and I remained.

But we couldn't, could we? The world was watching, ravenous, ready to devour us.

There was no hiding from those predatory eyes.

My heart broke as I pushed past Ariel and stood beside my little brother. I avoided Gloria's eyes, her questions. In a few minutes the area was swarming with cops and EMTs.

The first officer to arrive—Acosta—let us sit in the back of his patrol car. Gloria drove her weeping son away.

Once detectives were on the scene, Officer Acosta took us back to the projects, jotted down Nando's statement.

Then he drove away, and that was that.

Ariel and I didn't speak again.

~~~~~

Only a few weeks later, Linda Pompa became my "beard." She was a rocker girl at PSJA High School. One of her teeth was rimmed in gold, she loved Joan Jett, and she had been trying to get me to go out with her since Diana had dumped me in front of the auditorium last school year. I asked her to be my girlfriend, started walking her to class. Made out with her behind the choir room.

Ariel watched from afar, eyes red with weeping, until one day he didn't anymore.

I came home to find that he and his mother had moved away. Back to California, I supposed, or maybe another small town beyond the clutches of his abusive father.

I broke up with Linda immediately. My heart wasn't hers.

~~~

For months afterward I couldn't sleep. I would close my eyes and see those legs, that dusty, weed-entangled torso.

Every night, the body would shudder and sit up.

I *wish* I could tell you that it was a zombie, hungering for my flesh . . .

But it had the face of my beloved, eyes full of tears.

Beautiful flesh covered in gaping wounds.

Lying there in my mind, discarded and decaying.

I was trapped in the weeds of my cowardice, watching his features fade from my memory into silent oblivion.

To keep the undead shell of that love alive, I slowly fed it my soul.

~~~

Late one night, a week before graduation, the phone rang. I could hear Robert Smith crooning "Torture" in the background.

"Ariel?" I asked.

There was a sob.

"Don't hang up, please," I begged, my chest aching. "I . . . I'm so sorry."

He cleared his throat. "You hurt me, Oscar. Bad."

Clenching my free hand into a fist, I nodded though he couldn't see me. "I was afraid to risk your life. Afraid to risk mine. As much as I wish I could, I can't be you. I'm not brave enough. Not strong enough."

Ariel sighed. "One day, Oscar. One day you'll find the strength. The world will change, sweet boy. Hang in there."

The line went dead. I hit *69 to call him back, but I got a busy signal.

Ariel had left my life forever.

But his words echoed in my heart. The nightmares ended. Not quite two years later, at UT Pan American, surrounded by other queer kids, I gathered the courage to be who I am.

And I fell in love with a boy again.

IS HALF MEXICAN-AMERICAN, MEX-ICAN ENOUGH?

by **ALEX TEMBLADOR**

*N*o hablo español.

For a long time, these three words were my least favorite words in any language.

They didn't just mean "I can't speak Spanish." They meant "I can't understand you. I can't speak the language that my ancestors and your ancestors spoke."

It felt like a forever apology, one that never ends, for once you begin saying it, the result never changes—no matter the minor in Spanish you worked hard to get, or how often you listen to the Duolingo podcast, or even if you turn on the Spanish subtitles on Netflix.

Instead of "I can't speak Spanish," I felt like I was saying, "Sorry, I'm not Mexican-American enough."

I grew up in Wichita Falls, Texas, an eight-hour drive from the border city of Laredo, Texas, where my Mexican-American father was born. His mother and father met at the Laredo base, but after marrying, my grandfather was transferred to the base in Wichita Falls, where my father and his three siblings grew up in a poor white neighborhood far from the area of town where the Latinos lived.

My grandfather didn't grow up in California speaking Spanish. While his parents spoke the language, they only spoke it with other adults and behind closed doors. Most everyone in their neighborhood spoke English. On his side of the family, I'm between fourth- and fifth-generation American, depending on what parentage you trace.

My grandmother, a second- or third-generation American, grew up in a community dominated by Mexican and Mexican-American cultures in Laredo, Texas, speaking both Spanish and English. Her father was a WWII prisoner of war, proud of his military service and his country, America. And so, upon the move to Wichita Falls and my grandmother's entry into the military world, she made a choice not to teach her children Spanish, allowing them to dive fully into a white American culture of bologna sandwiches, football, and popular music.

My father married my mother, a blonde-haired, blue-eyed Caucasian woman from Wichita Falls, and soon after, I was born. While my father had a full Mexican-American daughter from a previous marriage, I was his first Mixed child, both Mexican-American and white, and a few years later my brother would also be born with this identity.

I grew up Mixed American, which is to say that I grew up straddling two cultures: white American and Mexican-American. On my Mexican side, we had tamales at Christmas, played lotería at family gatherings, and danced the cumbia at weddings. On my white side, my mother made biscuits and gravy every Sunday and we gathered often for American sporting events like baseball and football.

This Mixed childhood was wonderful, and most of the time I lived blissfully in the middle ground of my cultures, except for the occasional trips we took to Laredo, Texas. It was there that I had some inkling that I was different from my Mexican-American cousins, aunts, and uncles. But the trips were quick, so I never took the time to understand what I felt.

It wasn't until I went to college that I ever took interest in my Mexican-American identity.

The University of Louisiana at Monroe sits in northeast Louisiana, and when I attended ten years ago, I could probably count the number of Latino students on my fingers and toes. The community has diversified since then, but during my three years at the university, it had nowhere near the diversity that I'd experienced in Texas, or even on visits to New Orleans.

The week before my freshman year started, a Black man born and raised in Louisiana asked my boyfriend at the time (who was also Black, but from my hometown in Texas), "Oh, you're dating a white girl?"

Despite a thin, athletically built white mother who has blonde hair and blue eyes, I am a woman with dark brown hair, large thighs, full breasts, and tan skin with undertones of red in the summer and yellow in the winter. I had never been mistaken as "a white girl" before, and no one beyond Monroe,

Louisiana, has ever labeled me as such (I've been mistaken for everything from Native American to various Latino identities, Middle Eastern, East Asian, various Mixed race combinations, and occasionally Pacific Islander or Black. "What are you?" is a commonly posed question).

My boyfriend and I looked at each other, confused, because where we came from there were large Mexican-American and Mixed populations, and I was visually recognized in our hometown as such. Neither one of us knew how to respond immediately, but eventually my boyfriend said, "She's Mexican, dude."

During my three years of college, I faced similar experiences among the Black populations who saw me as white, since I wasn't Black. The white populations saw me as "brownish," though they understood enough to know I wasn't Black but wasn't fully white, either, and generally treated me as such. I didn't fit in with the locals, and I missed the sight of Mexicans and Latinos and the availability of Mexican food and cultural experiences that I was used to in Texas.

At the time, discussions about race and identity weren't common in the news or society, much less on campus or in the conservative city of Monroe. As the years passed and my understanding of race and identity increased, I came to understand that the perspective of my racial and ethnic identity by Louisianans—both Black and white—was perhaps a result of colorism born of the state's fraught history with slavery. Race was determined by the ruling class—white citizens—who used things like the paper bag test to determine who was Black and who was not. Nothing existed in the middle ground—much less the brownness of Latinos, who weren't predominantly present in the state and did not require their own rules of segregation or classifications, as occurred in Texas. Such perspectives remained long after rules like the paper bag test were abolished.

During my undergraduate studies, I felt untethered, floating through a community where my identity didn't have its own space (beyond the one Mexican restaurant, whose notoriety in the city was a place to go drink on Cinco de Mayo). I craved my Mexican-American heritage in a way that I hadn't before, and I was determined to connect myself with it so that no matter where I went in the world—whether there were Latino populations or not—I wouldn't float off again.

When I left Louisiana in 2011 and moved to Oklahoma City for graduate school, a place with a far larger Latino population, I was eager to learn more about my Mexican-American heritage, integrate myself into the community in a way I never had before, claim this part of myself, and figure out what exactly it meant to be "Mexican-American."

My cultural exploration took many forms, such as the writing of my first novel, *Secrets of the Casa Rosada*, which follows a sixteen-year-old exploring her Mexican-American identity in Laredo, Texas. Just as my main character, Martha, comes to learn, discovering my Mexican-American side was not as easy as I would have liked.

Among the Mexican and Latino friends that I made in Oklahoma City, I felt out of place, like a visitor passing through. I didn't understand some of their cultural references

or everything they said in Spanish. Anxiety and fear of embarrassment arose inside me when I went to all-Latino bars and
dance clubs and tried bachata for the first time. I was grateful
to be invited to barbacoa cookouts in backyards but felt like an
idiot for not really knowing what barbacoa was or how it was
cooked, even though I'd eaten it many times before.

I was shocked to learn about colorism within the community, and the politics and social nuances between Mexicans and
other Latino peoples, and for the first time, I gained insight into
the experiences of Latino immigrants, gender roles in Latino
households, and so much more. I was trying to become closer to
my heritage, but the more I learned, the more I struggled, suddenly realizing how much privilege and opportunity I'd been
afforded in my life being only half Mexican-American.

Though I was always curious and grateful for those Latinos
who openly welcomed my exploration of identity, secretly, hot
shame filled me inside, reminding me that I had taken so long to
learn all these things.

My shame worsened at times with occasional statements like
"You can't speak Spanish? Then you're not Mexican."

Despite all the exploration into my identity—whether it was
the fictional and historical books I read by Mexican-American
authors, the new foods I tried and made at home, the family
history I looked into, or the dances and cultural celebrations I
took part in—none of it seemed to be enough because I did not
know Spanish.

This is where I began to hate the phrase *No hablo español*.

Although I had argued that "One's ability to speak a language does not determine their cultural background," something inside me wondered if I was wrong.

I took those feelings of shame with me when I visited Mexico and other Latin American countries or met individuals who wished to speak to me in Spanish. Even now, over six years, two more moves, and one book published, no matter how "good" of a Mexican-American I try to be, that nagging little Spanish-speaking shame bubble likes to raise its head every once in a while, and I can't seem to pop it out of existence.

In early 2019, I was on a panel at TeenBookCon in Houston and a Mexican-American teen said, "I'm Mexican-American. I'm proud to be Mexican and I'm proud to be American, but sometimes I don't feel like [people] see that." I could relate.

The hyphenated experience of being Mexican-American is wrought with so much confusion, especially among Mexicans who are second- or third-generation Americans. Even as their parents instill Mexican history and culture in them, immersing themselves in their American heritage is inevitable. It creates this identity where they feel too American for the Mexicans and too Mexican for the Americans. As the character of Abraham Quintanilla, the father of famed Tejano singer Selena, said in the film, "We gotta prove to the Mexicans how Mexican we are, and we gotta prove to the Americans how American we are."

Perhaps, because I am Mixed, I'm in a unique place where I can understand these feelings better than most.

I will always be Mexican-American and white American. My identity is doubly hyphenated. As I've grown older, I've felt more at home in my Mixed identity because I've accepted that

I exist in the in-between, in two places at once. Perhaps that is what being Mexican-American is too.

Throughout the years I've wondered: does being half Mexican-American make me Mexican enough?

Ironically, my question is answered each time a person of Mexican heritage speaks to me in Spanish.

Mexican-Americans see me and feel that I am like them. They want to connect with me in a beautiful language that feels like home. They want to speak to me about their fears, their hopes, their interests, or just to ask for directions. They ignore my nervousness when I reply shakily in Spanish and are patient enough to allow me to stumble over the first few sentences, or change language tactics completely when I reply, "Lo siento, no entiendo."

They don't care if I'm half white because I'm half Mexican-American. Just like other Mexican-Americans, I'm angry when Latinos are targets of violence or discrimination. Just like other Mexican-Americans, I rejoice when I see a book published that showcases the Mexican-American identity, get too competitive during games of lotería, have serious opinions about the best menudo and tacos in town, and feel the need to move, clap, and dance when I hear a Mexican corrido.

As I grow older, I myself have started to experience some subtle and not-so-subtle forms of bias and discrimination because of my Mexican-American heritage—something I don't recall experiencing as a kid or even as a young adult, changing my perspective considerably as I enter my thirties.

Having said all this, I, too, love the diversity of American music, sports, art, history, food, cities, and culture. I can move between the two cultures just as easily as I can my own personal racial and ethnic heritage—even if it comes with some uncomfortable moments at times. Because of this, I now identify as Mixed Latinx, or "Mixed," with the added explanation of "half Mexican, half white."

No hablo español aren't my three least favorite words anymore. And even though my first instinct is to say them and free myself of the embarrassment of fumbling through the Spanish language, I don't.

Sitting in my discomfort as I push past my nervousness is part of what it means for me to be Mexican-American.

So that's what I do.

SUNFLOWER

by **AIDA SALAZAR**

I'm in the barbershop when I hear it. It's so familiar, it hurts. So I do the only thing I can. I pull out my phone, and I let it all go.

Analicia cheated on me last week, so I broke up with her. See, I never meant to be a sixth-grade boyfriend, especially in the first days of middle school. I mean, who does that anyway? No one, I mean, no one in sixth grade even has a clue which way homeroom is or who their friend group should or should not be, or which bathroom is the most private to drop a deuce in when nature calls. All this is to say that it wasn't entirely my fault. We met before I even got to middle school, when I least expected it. Like playing piano, timing is everything.

I was seriously minding my business, just being a fifth grader in outdoor school and acting like a goof on the playground near the lake. Panzas and I were doing our best Miles Morales imitations, timing each other to see who would make it across the monkey bars fastest, when I felt it. The pull of watching eyes. Sounds creepy, I know, but it was less skin-crawly and more, I don't know, magnetic. So obviously, I turned my sweaty head and there she was—a girl with dark brown hair and honey hazel skin and cheeks so bright and round, they looked like peaches— just staring. She smiled at me, and I froze right in my tracks. I wasn't entirely sure if it was me who she meant to smile at, but in case it was, I wasn't going to move. I mean, I couldn't. I even stopped clocking Panzas, who huffed as he bounced off the monkey bars and came barreling toward me asking, "Lalo, dude, what's my time?" But I didn't answer him because I was straight frozen. Like freeze-tag frozen. If it hadn't been for Panzas looking at how spaced out I was and shoving me so hard that I fell back and landed in the sand, I probably would have still been there, completely helado.

She was sitting by the swing set, holding a pencil and an over-sized sketchbook on her lap. My mind went racing through all the possibilities. Was she drawing me? Was I annoying her and was this actually a stink eye? Or was she just looking beyond me at the green murky lake water that was basically a huge toilet for all the ducks and geese that crowded Lake Merritt? Then she smiled. It was one of those too-good-to-be-true, sparkle-on-the-teeth kind of smiles, too. I think my jaw dropped, because I was absolutely certain that she *was* smiling at me. She couldn't have been smiling at Panzas, who had his back to her, clueless that she was even there, and who, by this time, was jumping all over me, digging me deeper into the sand and screaming "dogpile!" like a wild call to our other classmates. That shining smile was all the fuel I needed to shoot him off me and jump to my feet and smile back.

Then, clearly still under the control of her pull, I made a beeline for the open swing right next to her. Not even Chava, the pushiest kid in school, could beat me to it. A trailing group of kids yelled behind me, all wanting to get there first. They were loud, there was sand kicking up everywhere, and the sky couldn't have been more blue, but somehow, somehow, the swirl of my entire playground world came to one finite focus point of glimmering quiet—her sweet sunflower face.

I may have tripped over the first words I ever said to her. "Uh, what are you drawing?"

"My little brother on the swing. You wanna see?"

I answered with an idiotic "Nice!" when I peeked over her shoulder to see that she was a really good drawer. Like, super talented and all that. Then she smiled again and literally, my heart shot out of my chest like an out-of-control boomerang and zoomed back in three seconds. No one ever explained that something so outrageous could happen to me. I sure as heck didn't know that moment would eventually lead me to be her boyfriend. And not just any boyfriend, but her first, and she my first girlfriend, and that eventually she would do me wrong the way she did.

Analicia's voice was in the key of F. Definitely in F. How do I—a snot-nosed twelve-year-old—know that? Well, I've got perfect pitch, and I can't help but match the pitch of everything I hear to its note. Playing piano did that to me, and I've been playing for so long, it comes second nature. Amá says I shouldn't advertise "my talent," but whatever, I don't think anyone my age really cares about stuff like that.

Anyhow, a sunflower of a girl made me go bonkers with just her smile and her key-of-F voice. It's true. See, I didn't have a phone because I was in the fifth grade and Amá wasn't about to give me one, but Analicia did because it turned out she was a year older than me. Yeah, I know, it's insane, she's an older woman. But I didn't text her. I couldn't. What was I going to do? Use Amá's cell phone? So, I just let it go because it was too wild for me to believe that sort of thing happened to people— especially to tall and skinny piano-playing fifth-grade nerds like me. And even though I scanned the park for her every day when I came to outdoor school and we happened to be on the playground, I didn't see her there again.

It wasn't until a year later, on the first day of middle school, that I walked into the cafeteria and saw someone with a yellow glow around her. It was Analicia! She waved me over! I made another beeline for her. I'm telling you, that's the kind of power her smile had over me. And with as little as a "Hey, Lalo! I thought I'd never see you again!" we began.

Amá had folded and finally given me a phone by that point, so I texted Analicia before lunch and asked if she wanted to sit together in the cafeteria. By the end of the day, she was my girlfriend and the kids at school were berserk with gossip about the "new couple."

"It's the first day of sixth grade! Why is this even happening?" Panzas basically yelled at me as we walked out the front doors of school. I didn't expect him to understand. Which was fine. He had never been pulled by a magnetic sunflower before.

That night, over text, I found out that Analicia was a Marvel nerd, like me, and she didn't like DC as much; that she practiced martial arts, like me; she liked hip-hop musicals, like me; and she drew anime, my absolute favorite. Like, how could she be more perfect? She couldn't.

So, I really liked to hold her hand and drape my arm over her shoulder while we walked. I mean, it made me feel electric. Though I did wonder all the time about what it would feel like to kiss her, I was too chicken to try. Then, this one time, as I was walking her to class, out of nowhere, *she* kissed *me*. I didn't have to do a thing. *She* was the one who held me by the face and planted a big fat wet one right on my lips. I was pan dorado. Toast—all crispy and dark on the edges and overdone. I was so done.

I really thought everything was going great. We were texting all the time, spending most of our lunch periods together except when Panzas and the kids in band would make me practice with them. I'd send her video recordings of me playing her favorite songs on the piano. She sent me drawings. Our moms even met at a PTA meeting and actually planned supervised "playdates" for us on the weekend because they didn't have a clue about the smooching. Though, in all fairness, Amá *would* say, "It's nice you have a sweetie," and wink at me, which made me believe that she knew something was up.

Anyway, we were locked in and it felt like I was a walking ignited Tesla machine. Then, two months in, Panzas slipped me a note during math: *Meet me at your locker at lunch. Come alone. Code word: burrito!!!* What worried me about that note was the code word. It was something Panzas and I used only in very extreme cases; *burrito* meant business. Cosa seria. When I got to my locker, Panzas's face was all pruned up. And then he said, "Dude, Chava likes Analicia."

"Oh yeah. So? Who can blame him?"

"Nah, Lalo, he ain't kidding. He says he's going to take her from you and everything."

"Well, I'd like to see him try," I said, because she was a whole human and wasn't something to be taken. Plus, I was feeling pretty confident that nothing, absolutely nothing in the whole universe, could destroy what Analicia and I had.

When I let Analicia know what Panzas said, she confessed that Chava *had* been texting her and telling her all sorts of sweet things. She showed me how she was trying to keep it cool with him and had gently turned him down, which was a relief. The next day though, when Analicia and I were in the hall and Chava was walking by and looked our way, I gave him a dirty look. But later, Ms. Dominguez, the dean, called me in because Chava reported me for being "aggressive"! Imagine, for a dirty look? The dingus. Ms. Dominguez let me go because I told her I never said a word to the kid and he couldn't prove a thing. What I didn't say to Ms. Dominguez was that Chava was right to call me out—he knew that I was sending him a message that he better not even *think* about Analicia.

Things seemed to chill after that. Maybe my laser mean face had put him off. But it didn't last long; Chava wasn't done.

The next day he started texting nasty emojis to Analicia, like eggplants and drooling faces and other messed-up things like, I don't know why I even liked you, you aren't that smart. She sent me screenshots of those texts. After school I went looking for Chava. I was not going to let him get away with being abusive and sucio to Analicia. Lucky for him, I didn't find him. I didn't find him the next day, either, because he didn't come to school. Panzas said he heard Chava's parents were splitting up and so he was going to have to move or something. Whatever. I wasn't going to let him off the hook.

Analicia let me jump on her phone and I texted Chava. It's Lalo. I've got Analicia's phone. We're showing this to Ms. Dominguez. I'm not sure if it was my threat, his parents' divorce, or what, but Analicia said he stopped texting her—así no más.

When Chava finally came back to school the following week, he acted like nothing had happened. Like Analicia and I didn't exist. I thought, *Good. Let's keep it that way.* But then Panzas handed me another *Code word: burrito* note. This time Panzas had a summons. Chava wanted me to meet him after school, to fight. *All right,* I thought, *I'm going to have to take him down once and for all.* Chava was literally a head shorter than me, so I knew it would be over with quickly. But we never made it to the fight. Ms. Dominguez got word of it, and she brought us both in for a restorative circle, which is just fancy speak for trying to make us squash it. At the circle, Chava's chest was all puffed out like he was a balloon or something. *Oh yeah,* I thought, *let me just pull out my phone and show Ms. Dominguez the kind of weasel he really is.* Before I could do that, though, Chava had *his* phone out and was showing Ms. Dominguez and me the love texts between him and Analicia! I couldn't believe what I was seeing. My girlfriend, the sunflower, actually liked this guy! She said there was something forbidden about Chava and that she liked the thrill of him. I mean, YUCK! I wanted to scream and pound his face in with a karate kick. I felt like my insides were burning up and melting. It was literally the worst.

So here I am, waiting at the barbershop to get a fade, and our song *has* to come on. Yeah, Analicia and I had a song. Big surprise. It's "Sunflower." From the *Spider-Man* soundtrack. I don't know how, but it starts filling my head with all of these memories about what it was like to be a sixth-grade boyfriend and feel electrified, so I just had to type it all into my phone. Maybe it's easier to write it down so all the static I've got built up inside has somewhere else to go. Or maybe it's because I miss her every time I hear that song.

LA MIGRA
by RENÉ SALDAÑA JR.

We're boys, so at the sight
of their white trucks stirring
up dust in the distance,
we scamper like cockroaches.
Just like that, in no minutes flat,
they're right up on us, the words
on the back panels easy to read:
US BORDER PATROL in green.

They step out the air-conditioned trucks,
men in green uniforms carrying guns
at the ready—Cowboys of the New West—
always on the lookout for mojaditos,
brown wetbacks, whose hair and skin and eyes
are brown like mine, whose crime is to want

to work in the fields alongside our mothers

and fathers, whose only dream it is

for their children to play marbles or

hopscotch with us—

all of us

free and brown and laughing,

all of us

running to hide from La Migra.

LA PRINCESA MILEIDY DOMINGUEZ

by **RUBÉN DEGOLLADO**

Thursday, My First Day of School

When you move schools—because your mother has to hustle no matter what and go where the chamba goes, or that one tía (not naming names) who said that family is family and you can sleep on the sofá as long as you need, but then starts giving you all side-eye when one month turns into two—it's like walking out before the end of one movie and walking in late to the next. You miss the important parts, the names of people, why they do what they do, whether they get what they want, and what happens to them in the end. I know most people won't get this reference and it will go *whoosh* right over their heads because they live their lives on puro rewind and fast-forward, streaming this and that, hitting the back button whenever they get bored. But they can always go back to it and see the parts they missed. *I* get it because my life is always being interrupted and I'm dependent on other people's Wi-Fi. The movie I keep walking out of is *Mileidy Dominguez: Just Getting Settled*, only to walk into *Mileidy Dominguez: La Interrumpida* as it's about to finish. And mind you, these are both dollar movies and not new releases.

Of course, I don't tell Miss Yoli, the clerk, any of this as I'm registering myself at Dennett CISD Ninth-Grade Campus, my third school this year on my world tour across Texas and the Rio Grande Valley. I want to tell Miss Yoli my theory about my life in movies because I can see she's a nice lady just by how she's kept me in her office instead of sending me away to the lobby to fill out paperwork and how she's not already attacking me about my mom not being here or going off about the purple streaks in my hair, which can't be dress-code approved. When we were up north, I had a school tell me to leave and not come back until my mother could come with me *and* I could show them that my hair was a "normal" color. This kept me out of school for weeks because it wouldn't wash out right away and Mama couldn't get off work. And there wasn't a papi to speak of, then or now.

I keep all that in and instead tell her this. I go, "Yes, my name is Mileidy Dominguez, pronounced Mi Lady." The clerk looks over her readers, her '80s salt-and-pepper wings of hair waving in the fan that she refuses to set in oscillate mode even though I wouldn't mind it because there're no vents that I can see.

"Mija," she says, "it's actually pronounced Milei*dy*." She really emphasizes that Spanish *d* in my name, the *d* that is pronounced like a hard *th*.

I like this clerk even if she won't share the fan with me. She needs it more.

"I actually go by Leidy, you know, because I don't want people thinking they own me even though that's my legal name. Like, I don't want them to say 'my' when they talk to me."

"*Leidy*, you're sure your mother can't come to fill out the forms?"

"Keep asking the questions, and we'll get to that truth together." Mama is working a new job at Stripes selling mostly cigarettes, cases of beer, and lottery tickets, and of course breakfast tacos in the morning as the viejos go to work. She can't get out of a shift because she'll lose her job, and I don't feel like telling Miss Yoli this because I want to be a woman of mystery for at least fifteen more minutes before she pulls out that form I hate.

She cracks a smile and takes a little sip of coffee from her cup. I'm the one interesting part of her morning.

"Do you have proof of residence? Like, where you live," she says, and something in her tone says that this is a question she's required to ask but doesn't necessarily care about.

"Nope, nel pastel."

"Who taught you that? I haven't heard that in a *long* time."

"Pues, who else, miss? My moms."

"Seriously, mija, you sound like a forty-year-old woman saying 'nel pastel.'"

"Um, thanks?" I say, and put the purple streak of hair behind my ear. I'm still surprised Miss Yoli hasn't asked me about my hair yet.

"I'm sorry, mija, I'm not making fun of you. It's just been a long time since I've heard that." I think to tell her that this is how Mama talks, teaching me the old ways, how people used to talk in the Valley, taking me to the places she went to when she was little because she wants me to know the history of her home now that we've moved back. I think that deep down somewhere inside her, because we don't have a lot of family, Mama is afraid that it will all end with her if she doesn't pass these things on to me. Since we never have a place we call home for long, we learned a long time ago to hold value in only a few objects we can take with us, things we must also be ready to let go of if we have to. This is why we carry most of our memories through words.

Holding our history in my center, knowing the old ways and words, helps me hold on to who I am, but it also helps with the viejitos. When I'm registering with counselors or the clerks, or when the assistant principals start threatening me with sus-pension or ISS because I violated dress code, missed too much school, talked back, or got into a fight with some girl who made fun of me one too many times, I use these words and throw them over the viejitos like a blanket. Help them reminisce under their colchita and think about the old days.

Ay, *mija*, they say. *You took me back. Now go to class and don't let me catch you doing that again.*

I go through the forms Miss Yoli hands me, filling out what I can while she takes her little sips of coffee, typing something, and clicking her mouse from time to time. Queen's a multi-tasker. I know the special form is coming, the one I don't want to fill out because this will determine the way Miss Yoli will look at me forever after.

She hands it to me and I have a decision to make. Do I fill it out honestly or use some address from anyone I know near the school, like maybe that tía I'm not going to name who just last night asked us again when we would be getting a place of our own. She gave us the side-eye and sucked her teeth when Mama said she was going to find something soon, that she's just trying to save up for the deposit. It is a simple question for most girls my age: Where do you sleep at night? You'd think the form would ask you, where do you live? Then I would fill it out: *With my mama.* Or if it said, do you have a home? *Yes, wherever my mama is.* But no, it says to best describe where the student (me, because I'm filling it out) sleeps. You are expected to put an X next to one of the lines below.

_____ In a home that the student's parent or legal guardian owns or rents
(I wish)

_____ In a place that does not have windows, doors, running water, heat, electricity, or is overcrowded
(Literally anywhere other than a house)

_____ Staying with a friend or relative because of loss of housing, economic hardship, or a similar reason
(Or your tía who's the queen of side-eye)

_____ In a shelter
(Mama will never allow it again after some stuff went down)

_____ In an unsheltered location, such as:

- A tent
- A car or truck
- A van
- An abandoned building
- On the streets
- At a campground
- In a park
- In a bus station or train station
- Other similar place
- (Thankfully, not for long, and not now)

_____ In a hotel or motel because of loss of housing or economic hardship
(Texas Inn being our favorite)

_____ In a transitional housing program
(Never been to one even though I'm always in transition)

Then the form goes into a whole section about you being homeless as a result of natural disasters like hurricanes, floods, tornadoes, wildfires, and "other," which I guess is where you would put things like a global pandemic, economic collapse, EMP/nuclear war, alien invasion, which, when I think about it, they should have a whole section for unnatural disasters and YouTube theories.

I decide to continue being a woman of mystery, so I put an X next to *other* and write in: *It depends.* Miss Yoli should love that.

I hand it over.

She looks at the form, and her eyes get tiny like an abuelita who's caught her grandbabies up to no good but at the same time wants to laugh at the mess they've made.

"Okay, Leidy, it says here *depends.* I'm not Walter Mercado, who can read your mind or tell the future. Wait, do you even know who that is?"

I circle my fingers over my core like my hand is circling the universe inside me, and say, " 'Paz, mucha paz, y sobre todo, mucho, mucho, mucho, mucho amor.' " And on the word *amor* I blow a chef's kiss at her and give a little wink. It was Walter's signature move, wishing his viewers much peace and love above all else (que en paz descance). The wink is my edit.

She screams and starts laughing and keeps going that way, the tears coming down, grabbing at her side because the laughing is giving her a cramp in the ribs. Then she hits the speaker, dials the phone, and says, "Hey, Esmer, you have to come here. You're not going to believe it," but this Esmer puts her on hold.

I say, "Hey, miss, can you turn up the hold music? It slaps." And I'm being serious. It really does.

"Ay, mija, you're so safada."

Esmer never comes back to the phone and finally Miss Yoli gives up. I already don't like Esmer for ghosting my girl like that.

She gets on the radio instead and says, "Yoli to counseling, come in."

They don't answer, and she says, "This is Yoli Esparza, Community and Schools Coordinator, to counseling, come in."

Miss Yoli is flexing by throwing out that title; she's more than a clerk. She's got the power. She winks at me and nods, letting me in on her power flex. My girl's a *coordinator*. A queen.

~

Counseling sets me up with a schedule and then they send me back to Community and Schools Coordination with Miss Yoli Esparza.

"Knock, knock, miss," I say as I stand outside the doorway of her office. It's something I've seen old people do instead of actually physically knocking on the door.

"Come in, come in, mija." She's looked at all of my paperwork, maybe made a few phone calls, and has coded me homeless just like at my last school: *staying with a friend or relative because of a loss of housing, economic hardship, or a similar reason*. I can hear it in her voice, how it's just a little softer than it was before.

"Mr. Puentes wants to meet with you."

"What did I do?"

"Oh, mija, it's okay. He does that with as many of the new students as he can whenever they register."

"Who's Mr. Puentes?"

"He's the principal, mija."

She walks me over to his empty office and sits me down in a padded leather chair in front of his desk. "He'll be here in a minute."

There are stacks and stacks of paper on every flat surface. On the shelf behind his desk, and on the walls everywhere, there are picture frames of football players wearing Dennett blue and gold, cheerleaders, ballet folklórico dancers, choir kids, band kids, orchestra kids, poetry performance kids with fluttering papers in their hands, their mouths captured mid-stanza, and crowds of kids from the '90s, '00s, and '10s, standing around Mr. Puentes and his different hair shades over the years, smiling into the cameras. I stand up to look at the panoramic photographs of classes gone by and peer into their tiny faces. It's funny how all of the brown faces like mine are the same over the years, just with different makeup and hair.

"Mija, thank you, thank you for coming in," Mr. Puentes says as he walks into the office, in a rush, slightly out of breath. "Siéntate, mija, this won't take long. I want to get you to second period, which is about to start." At my last school, a counselor told me that I could miss the whole day as long as I was there at 10:07 a.m. when they took attendance.

"Homeroom is attached to second period, mija, and I want to make sure you get a little tour of the school before you go to class. I have a question for you."

He takes a deep breath and settles. He's older than Miss Yoli, more white than gray in his mustache and hair, and he has a kind face. He does make his eyes little as he notices my purple streak, but he doesn't say anything.

And then he asks me something no teacher, administrator, or counselor has ever asked me.

"What do you dream about, mija?"

I pause for a second, stunned. Of all the things he could have asked me, I was not expecting this.

"You mean like in my dreams? Like how I always dream I'm

flying, and when I do fly, it's no biggie, and it's like something I've always known how to do, but have only forgotten?"

"That's beautiful, and you'll have to tell me about it later, but no, mija, what I mean to ask is, what do you want for your life? You're fifteen now, and you might not know yet and that's okay. I want you to know that here at Dennett Ninth-Grade Campus we do everything we can to help you fulfill your dreams and your potential. We are all about dreams here, mija."

"I want to go to college." I almost say it as a question because I'm not quite sure if that's what he wants to hear. Mama has always told me that the first thing that comes out of your mouth when someone asks you a question is what is in your heart. So this is what's in my heart: I want to go to college.

He slams the papers on his desk and says, "Eso, mija, eso. Yes, that's what we're all about here. ¡Ganas! In addition to that, I want you to be thinking beyond college and what comes after, what you want out of your life, your kids' lives if you want to have kids, and the generations after."

"Sir, I'm fifteen and it's not even ten o'clock in the morning."

"Ay, mija, you're a character. We'll talk more about this later. Think about it." He then pulls up his radio and calls counseling and asks for a student ambassador.

"Please send Brittney to escort Leidy to her class." While he holds the radio up to his ear, waiting for a response, he pulls at long imaginary hair, gestures his white eyebrows at my purple streak, and gives me a thumbs-up.

Brittney, a girl who takes turns being bored and amused by her job as a student ambassador, talks in monotone one minute but then her voice lifts and rises as she goes through the practiced part of her tour. It's spirit day and she's wearing a Dennett Mustangs T-shirt, intentionally ripped jeans, and tennies.

She walks me first to the Hall of Champions, where high up on the wall there are white vinyl banners with different school years in their titles. They're long white banners with the phrase *Banner of Champions*, and under one it says *Graduation Commitment: Class of 2024* and so on. On these banners are hundreds of signatures, in different colored Sharpies of kids who have committed to graduating with their class three years down the line.

"These are our Banners of Champions." Brittney says in this practiced presentational voice. She pushes up her glasses.

"Sounds like a bunch of superheroes."

Brittney snorts. "Where are you coming from?"

"Oh, I've been all over. I went to the Bears, the Bulldogs, the Greyhounds, the Cardinals."

"Well, welcome to the Mustangs."

As she is walking me to my class, we pass the entryway, and up high in the hallway is another banner. It says *Second Annual Quinceañera: A Night Among Princesses.*

I stop and say, "What's that all about?"

"That's our annual quince. Mr. Puentes started it last year when he found out a girl wasn't going to have a quinceañera. It's actually tomorrow tonight."

"Like a real quince?"

"Yeah, with a cena and a dance and chambelanes and everything."

It takes me back to my fifteenth birthday earlier in the year, when we were living at Casa de Palmas, paying for the motel room week by week. Mama had taken me to dinner at Taco Fiesta and we'd both had the plate lunch special: carne guisada, rice, and beans. A real feast for anyone, and the typical dinner they serve at quinceañeras. Mama had gotten a flan to go and we'd gone back to the room to do our favorite thing together: work on a puzzle. We had done many as a team, but the one that went with us everywhere was a thousand-piece puzzle of the movie poster for *Titanic*. We had completed that puzzle and taken it apart more times than I could count. It was Mama's favorite movie. I had memorized Leonardo's and Kate's faces. The place where their foreheads meet as they lean into each other is always the hardest because the colors are the same, but it is my favorite and the part I always save for last.

It is too late for my quinceañera now because it's already passed, and looking at that banner, something breaks in me.

"Are you okay, Leidy?"

"Yeah, I'm okay. I was just remembering my own quinceañera." Brittney smiles because she doesn't get what I'm saying. She thinks I'm talking about a dance, the dress, the presentation, all of the padrinos and madrinas, the regalos. Brittney can't even imagine because the way her pants are intentionally ripped and those expensive glasses, she probably got all of those things.

"What's the Wi-Fi password?" I ask.

"It's 'Collegebound@2022.' Why?"

"I want to send my mom a picture."

I get out my phone and start typing it in.

"Why don't you just use your network?"

I lie and say, "I can't get a signal." Truth is, I don't have a signal anywhere I go and I use calling and texting apps to send messages. My phone hasn't been activated since two moves ago.

I take pictures of the banner and of the quinceañera announcement and send it to my mom.

Mira, mama, I type, and the pictures send.

"Can anybody go to the quinceañera? I mean, do you need an invitation or anything?"

"Yeah, just ask Mr. Puentes. He lets all the kids go. I'll be there. I already had my quince with my parents in December, but I was going to go for the dancing. The huapangos are wild."

"So anyone can go?"

"Anyone with an invitation, and Mr. Puentes hands them out to anyone who asks."

"Do you have to dress up?"

"Some do and some don't. The quinceañeras go all out because they get their hair and makeup done by professionals in Dennett and in other towns, and wear dresses that are lent out or donated. I mean, they are legit and get their photos done and everything. But for us students, it can be as casual as you want. You should go, Leidy."

The bell for second period rings and kids start coming out into the halls. They look just like all the kids from the other schools I've been in on a spirit day, except there seem to be more boys representing takuache cuh, which is a style that is a mix between preppy and wannabe new narco—how they wear embroidered jeans, belt buckles, and boots with tight polo shirts. When they aren't wearing hats, their hair is always slicked down with baby bangs in the front. It's not really important, but I always pay attention to little things like that, always try to get the social layout of any new school I enter.

"Let me take you to your homeroom or Mr. Puentes is going to get on my case and give me the student leader talk."

My back pocket buzzes and it's Mama.

Ay, mija, I wish we could have done that for you. There is a crying emoji, and Mama's gotten good at capturing her mood with them. It's not something I do, get involved with anything at school like going to events, joining clubs, or making friends for long, but I decide I want to go. Even though I learned a long time ago not to make any school home and always try to remember that home is Mama, Brittney pretty much had me at *huapango*.

Can I go? I ask Mama.

The little dots are flashing too long, which usually means no. And I kind of actually hope she doesn't give me permission because then it will take it out of my hands to decide. The little dots disappear and I guess that is my answer. I am actually relieved. It's easy to act brave in front of adults, but I know if I get too close to anyone my age, either I or they will disappear.

"I can't go," I say, and try to sound disappointed.

"Well, maybe another time we can do something else," Brittney says. The enthusiasm in her voice is real, and I can tell she's not just saying it to say something.

It only makes things worse because I know if Mama's new job doesn't work out, if we don't get enough for a deposit for an apartment, we'll be moving schools again. That means that when I move again, Brittney and I will say we will keep in touch, when what we really mean is that we will text for a while, then follow each other's feeds, and our friendship will then be measured in likes and comments, and then not even that.

~~~~~~

The day is pretty laid-back, and I think I might even like all of my teachers and classes. No yellers or condescenders, thankfully. Brittney is in my math class at the end of the day, but I've been avoiding her because I don't want her brainstorming other ways I can go to the dance. Besides being uncomfortable because I don't know anyone, I'll only be sad to see all of those girls in their dresses and me and my unintentionally ripped jeans and basic black tee, and see what I'll never have. Who wants to put themselves through that? I have to accept that my quinceañera was only me and mama, carne guisada, flan, and a *Titanic* puzzle.

Brittney is in the back and sends me a text, **Yr mom change her mind about going?**

No.
Be fun. Txt her again.

I already tried, I text, half lying by not texting that I only tried that once. Mama hasn't responded, and she won't because she isn't allowed to be on her phone at work; she's afraid of losing her job and she has to be at that counter the whole time.

"Miss," Brittney says, "can the new student go talk to Mr. Puentes? It's very important. I'm asking as her student ambassador." Listen to Brittney flexing her title.

I look over and mouth the word *no*. What does she think she's doing?

The teacher, who is checking her email, looks at us both and points to her wrist. There are only ten minutes left in the class, and as each teacher has posted in their classroom, that is one of the norms: *bell-to-bell teaching (no leaving the last ten minutes).*

I don't want to leave early anyway. What is the point?

Friday, My Second Day of School

It's my second day as a Dennett Mustang and there are only two things on my mind: the quinceañera and the night before, when I waited as long as I could for Mama to come home before I finally went to bed. In my first-period class, Mrs. Perez, the teacher I didn't meet yesterday, has us free-write a poem, a paragraph, a story, for fifteen minutes. It's her "sponge activity," which I know is supposed to mean we are being absorbed into the learning, but with her I can tell it's to sponge up a little more silence so she can drink her cafecito and sit at her desk. Because I don't have any paper and don't want to ask anyone for some, I get out my half-sheet bus pass.

I write:

> When I "double up" with family or friends,
> I live in spaces within spaces within spaces.

The house → the room → my mind.

Each space smaller and smaller,

Like nesting dolls,

Until I am the smallest,

Invisible and quiet,

But conscious, always conscious of the air I occupy,

Our section of the refrigerator,

The fifteen-by-fifteen bedroom

I share with Mama.

Mama came in last night after

I was asleep.

And in the morning I kissed her forehead

While she was still sleeping,

Curled up on the single bed,

Trying to make herself small,

Sleeping on her side so she won't snore

Through the door,

Which I silently shut when I leave,

Before I can ask her about the quinceañera.

I spend the day with these words and go through my classes period by period, knowing the quinceañera is tonight, reminded by all the announcements they make about it throughout the day.

The bell finally rings and I head out the front door to catch my bus, the half slip of paper in my hand from the day before telling me which route I am supposed to take, my poem written on the back side. I see crowds of girls heading to the band room where they're supposedly getting their hair and makeup done. The girls' locker room has been turned into a final fitting for their quinceañera dresses, all of which have been donated.

I'm standing out there in the front with the other kids and the vice principals holding their radios and shouting over the sound of the diesel engines and all of the after-school chaos, when I hear Miss Yoli calling to me from the main door.

"Leidy!"

I walk over to her and say, "I'm going to miss my bus." I just want to get out of there.

She ignores me and sings, "Leidy!"

I roll my eyes.

"Ah," she says, and sticks out just the tip of her tongue. "You probably never heard that song, have you?"

"Oh, Miss, of course I have. Kenny Rogers. It's an old joke, Miss. Sorry I can't talk right now, but I have to go."

"Anyway, mija, Mr. Puentes wants to speak to you. We'll hold the bus if we have to, but he wants to talk to you real quick."

I go through my quiet day, think about every word I spoke, every eye movement, every class I went to, and make sure that I haven't done anything to get me a discipline referral.

Miss Yoli walks me in and tells me to have a seat. She goes over to stand in the front office with Miss Esmer, where they are talking quietly like the adults do when they don't want the students to hear what they're saying. She keeps checking her watch, and I wonder if she's helping with the quinceañera. Brittney is working after school as a student aide, stamping what looks like announcements that will be sent home at some point. She throws me a peace sign and winks as if she's posing for a selfie.

Then Miss Yoli gestures to Miss Esmer for her to turn around and see me by pointing her chin and eyebrows my way. She brings her hand in front of her body and swirls it around like Walter Mercado, the old TV psychic, and then blows me a chef's kiss like she's approving of a fine meal.

"'Mucho, mucho, mucho paz y sobre todo, amor,'" I say back to her like Walter always used to say at the end of every episode.

They both start laughing. Miss Yoli then makes another announcement, telling all of the quinceañeras to go to the band room for makeup and hair, and the JROTC and Grupo Imagen to report to the small gym, that this is their final reminder. JROTC?

Mr. Puentes opens the door and waves me inside. He's smiling and twirling a lanyard of keys around his hand, so that's a good sign. Maybe I'm not in trouble.

When I walk in, there are even more white binders and papers on his desk, *While You Were Out* memos taped to his computer screen, and a blinking red light on his phone.

"Siéntate, mija, siéntate, I have something for you."

I sit down, and he hands me a glossy card with a pointy lavender princess hat on it. It reads:

Dennett Ninth-Grade Campus Second Annual Quinceañera
Join Us for a Celebration
In Honor of the Quinceañeras of the Class of 2025
Friday, May 6

Six p.m.
Presentation / Presentación
Blessing / Bendición
Dinner / Cena
Dance / Baile

"Ay, gracias, sir, thank you. Brittney told me about it. I texted my mom about going as a guest and she didn't text back, so I can't go. I really appreciate it, sir."

"No, mija, you don't understand."

"Yes, sir, it's tonight. I saw all the banners; they told me about it. But I can't go."

I get up to leave before I start crying.

"No, mija, listen."

"It's okay, sir. I hope everyone has a good time. I'll keep this as a souvenir," I say, and hold up the pretty invitation.

"Mija, will you just listen? Por favor." I wish he would stop calling me mija because it would make this easier.

"Mija, your mama called and wanted to know more about the quinceañera."

"You mean she called the school?"

"Yes, mija, and before she asked any more questions, I told her you could go if she was okay with it and if you wanted to."

"That's great, sir, but I don't really want to."

"Ay, mija." Mr. Puentes lifts his hands up, presumably to heaven. "What I'm trying to tell you is that you are a quinceañera and I don't care if you didn't start the school year with us. You are one of ours now, mija, even if you didn't join the

Mustang family until yesterday. And we want you to have this. Miss Yoli and I have been making calls to the parent activity club and the dress madrinas. Normally, we start working on the list at the beginning of the year, getting all of the girls fitted and matched with a dress, but as soon as your mother called, all of the madrinas in the community came together to find you the right dress. Miss Yoli says you're about her daughter's size and they went from there."

"But, but, but . . ." I can't get the words out. What I want to say is, *But it's too late. But it's tonight. But I already had my quinceañera. But I can't accept this.* What does come out are the lágrimas—happy but sad tears that catch me by surprise—ones I don't know what to do with. I didn't wake up planning to cry today.

"Leidy," Miss Yoli, Esmer, and Brittney sing in the doorway.

Mr. Puentes says, "I hope that's okay, mija. Your mother really wanted you to go and was excited."

I put my face in my hands because I don't know what else to do.

Miss Yoli speaks and her voice starts out shaky like she wants to cry too, but steadies itself as she goes into power mode.

"Okay, mija, apúrate. Vámonos, come on. It's time to get you ready for your quinceañera. All of the other girls are already in hair and makeup and the guests will be here soon. The madrinas are waiting for you."

Brittney pulls me by the hand, and even though I've only known her for less than two days, I let her pull me along. She can't stop smiling and making these little hop skips down the hallway. I still don't know if she's for real, because who acts like that, is enthusiastic for a girl she just met? You'd think it was her quinceañera. Maybe that's why she's captain of the Student Ambassador Club.

Miss Yoli walks ahead of us down the nearly empty hall, and she takes us to the band room.

I walk in and there, sitting in rows of chairs, are the other quinceañeras already getting their makeup done. The mood is festive and they're playing music, but not too loud, as I can also hear the girls talking to the stylists, who range in age from señoras who are probably mom volunteers to professionals donating their time. A stylish petite doña in her forties, makeup done in a modern chola look, walks among them, obviously in charge. She checks in at each station and talks to the stylists, giving them pointers while touching the hand of each girl almost like she's giving them her blessing.

Brittney and Miss Yoli walk me over to an empty band chair where I see a young rockabilly stylist slapping a cape over the back. She smiles at me, and with her black-framed glasses, carefully applied makeup, real tattoo sleeve of patterns and flowers, and red bandanna in her hair, she's more like a makeup tutorial artist than a señora they begged to do makeup for us girls.

"Oh, I love her," she says, putting my face in her hands. "My name is Beatriz, and we're going to have so much fun. I promise you, mamas."

Beatriz goes to work and narrates the whole time, telling me exactly what she's doing because I don't have a mirror to see.

I don't normally wear a lot of makeup and have never felt I needed to. I don't even know what to say. This is all happening so fast and I keep my eyes closed most of the time. Her words come in and out as her hands flutter over me with pencils and brushes and fingertips. Her words start to become a poetry of their own and they all come together in a combination of details and encouragement. *Eyebrow pencil to fill in the eyebrows. They're already such pretty cejas. Concealer, light sand, just a little for the base. Want your beautiful eyes to pop. Brush, then finger blend. Oh, mamas, you're beautiful. You have a face made for the soft glam palette. Accent your inner corners, but no harsh lines. Shimmery, mamas, shimmery. Burnt orange. Dark brown. Transition color. Pero no harsh lines. It's all about the blending. Glitter and glow. Do you want wings? Of course you do. Foundation. Beauty blender. More concealer. Bronzer. Now for the mascara. Oh perfecto, I can't wait for you to see. Some blush for you but just a little. Highlights so you glow, mija. Some lip pencil. Color pop. Satin finish.*

"Now open your eyes, mamas," Beatriz says, and busts out a hand mirror in front of me.

Before my eyes is another girl who is me, but not quite me. I have no words. Miss Yoli holds her hands together like she's praying. Of course Brittney takes a picture. This other girl who is not me, but is increasingly becoming me, is all those shades blending into each other where they're supposed to, but also popping. I am glowing. My eyes start to pool and I try to keep it together. It's like my recurring dream when I suddenly remember I can fly. This girl I see before me was always there.

Beatriz takes a tissue and lightly dabs over my lashes.

"Leidy, listen to me, mamas. You were beautiful before, and you are beautiful now. The makeup doesn't change anything. It's just showing a different side of you none of these people have seen. Princesa, today and forever. Now for your hair and your corona!"

~~~~

When I'm all done, and I'm wearing my crown, my hair topped high in a bun with curls coming down thanks to the curling wand Beatriz used and lots of bobby pins, Miss Yoli and Brittney take me to a room that says COMMUNITY ENGAGEMENT on the door. Brittney is doing her little hop, and I can't understand why she is so happy for me. Miss Yoli gathers all of the girls in front of the door and waits until we are all here.

"Okay, princesas. Your dresses are in here. Look for your name. Leidy, please come to the front." I make my way forward, and Miss Yoli winks at me as she unlocks the door.

In this white room with the blinds closed, I cannot believe what I see. There, on various racks, are too many quinceañera dresses to count in pink, purple, lavender, and green in tulle, satin, and chiffon, sparkles, rhinestones, droplets, and ribbons. Each dress has a pink paper with a girl's name safety pinned to it. There on the end, almost like it's in a place of honor, is my name, *Mileidy Dominguez*, written in cursive.

The rest of the girls rush forward, but I am planted there, unable to move.

Miss Yoli says, "Go ahead, mija, go look at your dress. We

hope you like it. We did our best with the time we had."

It is the deepest lavender, with embroidery and little rhine-stones on the bodice that look like stars. It is off the shoulder with an open back, which is showing a little more than I'm used to, but I can't deny it—this dress was made for me.

Miss Yoli caresses the lavender fabric and says, "To accen-tuate your hair, mija."

After all of the fussing to make our way to the locker room to change, and after we're all dressed, Brittney says, "Are you ready?"

I look around me and exhale. Am I ready? Am I really ready for all of this?

"I'm going to head in now. They are going to present you all."

I panic. "The chambelán?"

"It's all taken care of. They get the JROTC boys to escort the girls."

I must have a confused look on my face, because she says, "I know, I know. Just go with it. A lot of them are actually cute. I'll see you in there."

Miss Yoli says, "Ándale, muchachas, line up, line up, alpha-betical order. Let's go, let's go. Everyone is inside waiting. Mr. Puentes can't wait to present all of you."

The girls shuffle to their places, and I can tell they've prac-ticed this before. We are in line in the long hallway outside of the gym. There seem to be about thirty or so of us. The JROTC boys are in their uniforms on the other side of the hall, waiting for the girls to finish finding their places. Even though my hair is in perfect place, I'm standing there by myself, out of the line. I can't stop from curling a strand behind my ear because I'm nervous, and I don't have my phone to look at so I can pretend I'm bored with the whole thing. I have this fear that I won't have a chambelán and I'll be walking in there by myself.

Once all of the girls are in place, the JROTC go to their quinceañeras. I curl my hair behind my ear some more, as I'm still not in line and don't want someone to start asking who has a last name starting with D.

Miss Yoli yells, "Leidy, where are you? Where's Leidy?"

"I'm here!" The volume of my voice surprises me.

"Well, come over here, mija. This is your place."

The quinceañeras and the chambelanes smile and make way for me.

She brings a JROTC boy over to me, and even though he is cute, with a nice, nervous smile, he's shorter than me.

"Ay, mija, I did my best," says Miss Yoli.

The boy blushes, because no boy I've ever known wants to go out with a girl taller than him.

"It's okay, king," I tell him. "I'm good with it if you are."

He laughs and his laugh is real. "My name is Jaime, and I'm honored," he says, and like a gentleman, holds out his left arm for me to hook my hand through. It's like a real dama and chambelán, except this time I'm the quinceañera. Short king winks and smiles, and I notice he's got dimples and braces.

Past the open gym doors, I can hear Mr. Puentes announce us like he's on the radio. I can tell he lives for this, Mr. Fun and Games style.

"En este tiempo—at this time queremos presentar—we would like to present the quinceañeras del segundo anual— second annual Dennett Ninth-Grade Campus Quinceañera Celebration." People clap and cheer, and I wonder if anywhere else in Texas, or even the country, do people talk like Mr. Puentes with both languages on mash-up in one sentence like that.

The waltz song, "Balada para Adelina," fades in and the first girl steps through the door as soon as her name is called. It's this sweet, sad but hopeful, corny piano song, but we all love it. It's supposed to signify that we are leaving childhood and entering the adventure of the great beyond.

"Yaneli Anzaldúa." Clapping and cheering.

"Marlén Balderrama." Clapping and cheering.

It goes on like that until they get to the *D*s and I hear my name, "Mileidy Dominguez."

I straighten my crown, and as I walk through the doors under the pink streamers, I am handed a single rose. Jaime walks me all the way and adjusts his pace to mine. He lets go of me in the gentlest, sweetest way, and I walk to where all of the girls are lined up for presentation. There are stacks and stacks of fathers, mothers, abuelitas, and cousins taking pictures. Mama is not among them, but that would be too much for me to expect; I know she can't get out of work. I can't blame her for that. I'm here because she called the school, something she's never been comfortable doing.

As soon as all of us are lined up, Mr. Puentes says, "Comunidad, Community of Dennett, les presento—I present to you las quinceañeras. Please sit—y que se sienten por favor."

And they are all there at their tables, looking at me, at all of us in our glittery quinceañera beauty and promise, and I feel myself bursting free from spaces within spaces within spaces, the tiny nesting doll now becoming a living princess.

"I know we always thank the padrinos and madrinas at the end, pero antes de que se vayan—before anyone leaves quiero decir gracias, and muchos thank-yous. You made this possible. Thank you especially to the esteemed board members, teachers, paraprofessionals, all of the madrinas and padrinos who gave their time y donaciones, to Noche De Gala dress shop, Ernesto's Quick 'N' Clean, to Pastor Benny of Life in the Spirit Community Church, gracias—thank you for the cena! To Izquierdo and Sons Painting and Drywall for all of the decorations, thank you! But most especially, I want to publicly thank a lady who you all know and love."

He doesn't even get the name out because all of the kids start chanting, "Yoli, Yoli, Yoli, Yoli!"

"Ms. Esparza, could you please step forward so the students can recognize you?"

Miss Yoli gives this little half wave, and I can tell she's shy and doesn't want all of the attention on her.

"There are so many people to thank, but we also want to thank all the stylists of Karina's Touch of Beauty salon de belleza, who gave our girls the five-star treatment. Mrs. Karina Galán Izquierdo, can you please wave so we see you?"

Everyone looks around and finally we see the petite woman who was supervising in the band room. Doña looks so small, despite wearing tall heels and her hair high up in a bun. She's all style, wearing jeans and a white gauzy blouse. She waves. There's a lot of waving at this quinceañera.

Mr. Puentes says, "Now, Pastor Benny, if you would please come up and say the blessing."

This older bald man dressed in a black suit his chest is popping out of moves forward from where he's standing with the salon owner and the other community madrinas and padrinos.

He steps up to the podium as Mr. Puentes steps aside.

"Si me permites, Mr. Puentes, I'd like to read some Scripture."

"Por supuesto, of course, Pastor Benny."

He puts on some readers and pulls a little Bible out of his suit coat.

"A traditional reading for a young lady celebrating her quinceañera. 'Antes de formarte en el vientre ya te había elegido; antes de que nacieras, ya te había apartado, te había nombrado profeta para las naciones. Yo le respondí, ¡Ah, Señor mi Dios! ¡Soy muy joven, y no sé hablar! Pero el Señor me dijo, No digas, 'Soy muy joven, porque vas a ir adondequiera que yo te envíe, y vas a decir todo lo que yo te ordene.'"

Pastor Benny takes off his glasses and says, "Young ladies, you may not be prophets, or maybe you are, but for sure you are special and were known before you were born. This verse speaks to how you are princesses who are loved by your community, your school, and are called by nuestro Señor Jesucristo." Some of the quinceañeras and most of the adults at the tables cross themselves. He raises his arm and extends a hand toward us. "We love you and always want the best for you. May all of your days be blessed, and wherever you are sent into the world to do good, always remember this moment, your calling, your gente, and where you come from. And with that, Lord bless the food!"

Mr. Puentes says, "A las princesas, you are beautiful, hermosas, and we at Dennett Ninth-Grade Campus celebrate you and elevate you." The loudest clapping and cheering is for us, the princesas of Dennett.

~

The excitement starts to fade for me through dinner because all of the girls are sitting with their families, and like any party, they've invited their parents, abuelitas, tíos, and tías, and so their big round tables are full of loved ones.

Brittney sits next to me through dinner, and she must see me drawing back into myself because she says, "Hey, Leidy, did I tell you how beautiful you look? I mean, I know it's not all about looks, but you are radiant."

"Thank you, Brittney. I appreciate you being so nice," I say.

"I mean, for real, like I thought I looked good at my quince, but wow, just wow.

"Check it," she says, and starts going through her feed of pictures from her own quinceañera, showing me her hair, her cream-colored dress, her professionally done photos with a real photographer and a real camera. It's a little humblebrag on her part, but she's trying to be sweet because, other than her, I don't know anyone and I'm here alone.

Friends of hers come by and she introduces me, and takes selfies with them as they make their way past our table. She stays with me the whole time even though I can tell she wants to walk around and talk to her friends.

"You can go, Brittney. You don't have to stay here with me."

Brittney thinks about it for a second, and says, "Are you sure? Are you going to be okay?"

"Yes, Brittney, I'll be okay."

"Okay," she says. "But I'll be back. I'm just going to check on something."

She touches my hand, then leaves, and I am sitting at the table by myself, and this is always how I knew this would end.

The typical parts of the quinceañera, the presentation of the last doll from a girl's childhood, the changing of the shoes from tennies to high heels, won't be happening tonight. But there's one big thing that is on the order of events, the one thing I am dreading the most: the father-daughter dance. I haven't heard from my own father in years and it's only been Mama and me for as long as I can remember, but she's not here and won't be.

~~~~

As dinner winds down, I can barely touch the food in front of me because all it does is remind me of my sad little quinceañera with Mama where we ate only carne guisada; reminds me of Mama, who is not here now, and Brittney, who never made it back. Mr. Puentes comes up to the podium and announces what I've been afraid of.

"At this time, we will have the traditional dance." I feel like my soul is bleeding from me, pouring out all over the gym floor.

"But this is not a father-daughter dance. This is un baile de amor. Whoever is special to you, quinceañera, a father maybe, or a tía, your older brother who's always been there for you, your mother, grandmother. You decide."

The song, "No Crezcas Más," comes on, and even though I don't want to, the tears start to pool in my eyes because I see the quinceañeras with their fathers, some with their abuelitas, others holding hands with viejitos in their white Stetsons, taking the hand of their nietas, and I'm sitting there alone.

I close my eyes because I can't. I just can't. This can't be the end of my movie. *Mileidy Sits Alone Crying* can't be the title splashed across the screen while this sad song about a father not wanting his daughter to grow up starts just as the credits roll.

The song plays on and when it comes to that powerful part with the guitar and the rest of the instruments and the singer says, *"Por favor, no crezcas más,"* I decide it's time to leave.

And then I hear my name.

"Mileidy."

I open my eyes.

Standing in front of me is Mr. Puentes, holding out his hand, inviting me to the dance floor. But that's not it. I look past him and see a line at my table with others standing behind him. They all press in to see me. Mrs. Perez from English, and a few of my other teachers, Brittney with her hoppy expectation, Short King Jaime with his braces and dimples on full display, Beatriz, Miss Yoli, Esmer, all with their kind eyes and no pity in them, only love washing over me. They are all there, waiting and wanting to dance with me, gathered together by Brittney herself, and as each of them starts to blur because I can't hold it in anymore with these different tears, Mr. Puentes takes my hand and gently pulls me out of my seat and hands me his cell phone and puts it up next to my ear.

Even though I can barely hear, Mama says, "Mijita linda, aunque no puedo estar allí contigo, I am always with you and they are there for you now. We are all here for you, mi princesa."

And behind my eyes, as Mr. Puentes and my procession take me out to the dance floor for the baile de amor, I see the title of this uninterrupted new release of my life as the ending credits roll—

La Princesa Mileidy Dominguez: She Finally Gets What She Wants.

OJO

by SYLVIA SÁNCHEZ GARZA

Mami said she didn't believe, but when we would throw up or spike a fever and nothing seemed to explain why, she did. She would call Mina, our neighbor, to come over and check us and, unfortunately—do the dreaded "egg thing." Mina was a parent volunteer, a church volunteer, and a Girl Scout leader, but she specialized in ojo. My sisters and I hated it when she rubbed the egg on our belly. It was so weird. How can being stared at make you sick? None of it made sense, but we were used to it because sooner or later, "mal de ojo" happened without warning.

"Your grandpa used to say that some people had the power to look at someone in a certain way, and for no reason, they would end up curling over with pain."

"Like the evil eye?"

"It's more than that. It's a belief." Mami always said that she didn't believe in it, but we'd still get the egg thing, just to be sure—a dependable treatment.

Today I stay home from school crying so I won't have to face *her* again, but the experience is still stuck in my head; I can't stop thinking about it. I look out through my window and observe the sun disappearing behind the grayish clouds that look like they want to explode. Shaking uncontrollably, I cover my head with a blanket.

This past week was the worst. It started when I was transferred from my junior high English ELA class to the Honors English class. Mrs. Fritz approached with a smile as I shoved my sweaty hands into my red fringed jacket. I had worn it for protection against evil every single day since Mami bought it for me and embroidered a Virgen de Guadalupe on the inside. I took a deep breath as the teacher introduced me to my new classmates.

"Class, this is Suzy. She's here from English ELA. Let's welcome her."

The class smiled and pretended to work on their assignment, indifferent. Gracie, with long silky brown hair, wrapped her curls around her manicured index finger and stared at her curly locks, pushing them behind her ear, showing off her gold earrings and designer denim jacket. She glared at me then quickly looked away, shuffling her expensive mall-bought tennis shoes back and forth, scuffing the floor so I would notice them. I pulled on the fringes of my jacket that was just a tad too big for me and looked down at my worn boots.

After class, Gracie strolled up to me with her hand on her hip, stared me down, and then turned away. I followed her toward the door, where her friends were waiting. "¿Gracie, qué pasa? Did you wanna ask me something?"

"Listen, chicklet! I don't speak Spanish. I'm not like you. Who do you think you are, coming in here with *that* jacket? Where'd you get it anyway—the flea market?" My eyes got big, I didn't hear the insult for what it was.

"Haven't you ever been to la pulga?" I asked. "You can find all sorts of treasures there." On Saturdays we'd spend the entire day at the flea market, selling whatever we could for extra money and then shopping for everything from fruit to clothes and furniture.

"Are you kidding? I go to the mall. FYI, girlie, you don't belong in Honors English. Go back where you came from. Loser." Proud of herself, Gracie crossed her arms, laughing and glaring at me from head to toe like I was her worst enemy.

I was upset, but I didn't back down.

"This is the Valley," I said. "Hablamos en inglés y español. We can speak any language we want to; we can shop where we want to, and we're not into name brands like you. Besides, what's the big deal about my jacket?" I tried to keep my voice from shaking and tears from bursting out of my eyes.

"But why wear red? Are you trying to get noticed?" She signaled to her friends, who came over, oohing and ahhing over Gracie. They proudly listened to their leader.

Mrs. Fritz must have heard the whole conversation. But she only chose that moment to speak up.

"Don't worry about her," she said, brushing Gracie's words off. "She'll get over it."

Mrs. Fritz, surrounded by literature and poetry books, sat at the wooden desk, sipping her herbal tea, preparing for her next class to come in after lunch. Didn't she understand? Gracie point-blank hated me and wanted the entire class to hate me too. This "mean girl" acted like the newly crowned South Junior High School homecoming queen, prancing around with an invisible crown. Of course it upset me. She had insulted me right to my face.

Why me? I didn't do anything to her.

"Maybe she's a bit jealous." My teacher looked up at me from her steaming mug.

"Jealous? Jealous of what? She's not jealous. She's seems evil."

"Suzy, she doesn't understand you. Give her some time to get to know you. Our culture is new to her. Besides, I think she liked your jacket." Mrs. Fritz went back to sipping her tea.

"What? She made fun of my jacket. . . . Wait a minute. If she's jealous, isn't she supposed to touch my head or something? I don't want to get sick because she admired my jacket. She should at least touch my jacket, or else . . ." Mrs. Fritz stared at me again, not understanding,

For the next week, Gracie shot arrows at me with her eyes, and every time she talked to me, it made my stomach hurt. She wouldn't stop harassing me, following me wherever I went. She was always there, staring at me with *those* eyes. It was unnerving me.

Up until now, I've always loved school, but today I can't make myself go. I really don't feel well.

The door opens, and Mami walks in. She comes in close, places one hand on my shoulder, one on my forehead, and looks me smack-dab in my watery eyes.

"What's wrong, mijita? Te hicieron ojo?"

"That's not what's wrong with me, Mami. Please, don't call Mina. She'll come and start saying all this stuff in fast Spanish, then put the egg on me. I don't want that. My stomach hurts, and I want to throw up. I'm not going to school. The last thing I need right now is Mina talking weird with her hands and trying to cure me."

I know what the cause of all this is, but I can't tell Mami. She wouldn't understand. Besides, I'd prefer to handle my problems, including Gracie, on my own.

"Fine then, you feel warm, and you look pale. I think I'm going to take you to see what the doctor says." Dr. García, our family doctor, delivered all five of us, and Mami trusts him with her life. "And if I need to," she adds, "I'll call Mina."

I get on my jacket even though it is warm outside, slip on my boots, and pack myself into the blue monster mobile. It's an old used car with faded paint on each side. I hate this car. Everyone notices it, and it putters every time it turns on, which makes it even more embarrassing. Mami takes us to school in it, and it is torture. I always ask her to drop me off a block away so that no one can see me. All I need now is for Gracie to notice me getting out of that car.

I find myself lying down in the back seat, holding on to my stomach, thinking about why I didn't just stay in my ELA class.

We arrive at the doctor's office, and we wait with strangers in the waiting room. What's the point? Dr. García isn't going to help me. He doesn't have a medicine for me. But I sit there because I have no choice.

There's an older lady with a young man, perhaps her son, sitting on one side of the room. She's wearing a huge black sweater even though it's about a hundred degrees outside. Her perfectly braided silver hair must be twisted on top of her head at least four times. The deep wrinkles must represent all the problems throughout her life. She sits on the hard chair, mumbling to herself, wringing her hands with a rosario wrapped around her fingers. Her son is flipping through *Automobile* magazine with "Cars of the Month" on the cover. His eyes peer up and creep me out, but I pretend not to notice and then turn away.

On the other side of the small room is a young mom with five kids aged about three to ten. The mom's hair, held in place with a bulky clip, and her wrinkled, loose clothing make her appear much older than she probably is. Her pale face looks down at the floor with closed eyes. How can she possibly do it all? No wonder she's at the doctor's office.

To the right of the woman is a man, sitting alone, with a cough that sounds like a barking dog, wiping his mouth with his hands.

I shudder at the thought of sitting there among all these germs.

The soft music is playing, and it smells like Clorox has been splattered all over the floor and seats just minutes before we walked in. There's no place to lie down, so I lean over and rest my head on Mami's shoulder. After what seems to be hours, I doze off and dream about how I wish things could be for me.

"Suzy . . . ?"

Finally they call me. Mami and I go behind the mysterious closed door, and everyone in the waiting room stares at us with a look of jealousy. I almost feel guilty for being called, especially since the mom with all the kids is still out there. Now they are jumping from chair to chair while the mom keeps her head down. Maybe they should have called her first.

"Get on the scale."

The nurse doesn't mess around. I stand on the step and she moves the weight back and forth.

"Hmmm, you lost a little weight since last time, and that's with your jacket still on. You should be gaining, not losing."

"Really?"

"Ay, que niña es, no come."

"Follow me." The nurse takes us into a room. I shove off my boots, jump on the examining bed, lie back, and wait for the doctor.

"He'll be with you in a minute." After the nurse walks out, I listen to the voices that seep in through the wall. We sit and wait and wait and continue to wait in the small room, and I study the posters on the wall. There's one that details the human body, another one that shows a very detailed diagram of the stomach, including the digestive system. *Interesting*, I think as I try to read them while holding on to my own stomach. The wait seems like hours, and I stare at the ceiling. I wonder how many other sick people have lain on this very same examining table.

Finally the door opens. I sit up. "Cómo están? ¿Cómo está Tony?"

"Hola, Doctor. Estamos bien, nomas que esta niña . . ."

He turns his attention toward me and begins to check my eyes and mouth. He then checks my heart with his stethoscope and looks in my ears.

"Lie down, mijita." My eyes turn from side to side. I look at Mami, turn to Dr. García, then look at the wall. I take a deep breath and lie down, and he begins to press on my stomach. He listens to it with his stethoscope.

"Hmmm . . . Let's draw some blood and see."

The nurse comes in with her gloves and prepares to do her task with all the vials. She wraps a tourniquet around my arm and stabs me with a needle. In a second, it's done.

"You can rest in the waiting room."

Fine, we might as well wait in the holding pen, aka "the lobby"; we've already been here all day anyway. We go back into the blah waiting room, Mami picks up one of the *Good Housekeeping* magazines on the table, and I curl myself into a ball on the chair. The lady sitting across from us stares at me, and I can't help but think she might be the substitute teacher who we had the other day when Mrs. Fritz was out sick.

I look down at the floor and close my eyes. I get up to go to the bathroom. The lady keeps staring at me but doesn't say a word. She's making me think about all the issues at school, so I quickly walk away.

In the bathroom, I look at myself in the mirror. That only makes me feel worse. My face looks pale. Am I sick? I stick my finger in my mouth, trying to throw up and prove to Mami that I am sick, but nothing comes out. How can it? I haven't eaten. I wash my hands and walk into the holding pen. When I get back to my chair, the lady is gone. Thank God I don't have to look at her anymore.

"Suzy . . . ?"

Yes! They didn't forget about me. Mami and I stand up and head toward the door.

"Room number two, please. The doctor will be right there." Here we go again, another two hours before he comes in.

This time he surprises us. The doctor comes in just a few minutes later, with the nurse following. He looks over at Mami.

"Do you mind if I talk to Suzy privately?"

Mami looks at me, and I nod. Then she leaves the room, and the doctor sits on his stool and scoots closer to me, with the nurse standing behind him, taking notes.

"Mijita, I've known you all your life. If there is something that you need to talk about, you can talk to me. Is everything all right with you at home?"

"Yes."

"Is everything all right with you at school?

"Yes." No, not at all.

"Is there something that's bothering you?"

"No." Obviously, there is.

"Are you having problems with friends or kids at school?"

"No." You could say that.

"You know, you can always talk to a teacher, principal, or counselor if you need to."

"I know." Yeah, right.

"Well, then if there's nothing else you want to tell me. I guess your stomachache will pass."

He gives me one more moment to speak up, but I let it go by.

"Okay," he says. "Let me call your mami in."

He steps out, and I put my head down. How could I tell him? How could I tell him anything? He wouldn't understand. He fixes people with shots and medicine. He can't fix my problems.

Mami walks in and sits down.

"All the blood work is fine. I'll give Suzy a doctor's note so she can go back to school. If there's something else bothering her at any point, bring her back."

"Gracias, Doctor." Mami helps me down from the table and walks out of the room, stopping at the desk to pay.

"Well, Dr. García says everything is fine, Suzy. Do you need to tell me anything?"

"No." Another lie.

We weave past the blah waiting room with new faces sitting in the hard chairs waiting for their names to be called, then step out to the parking lot, where our monster mobile is. I lie down in the back seat, and we drive home.

"I still feel sick." I roll over as Mami turns back and looks at me with her eyes wrinkling up.

"Now I'll call Mina." As soon as we get home, I crawl into my bed.

"No se le quita el dolor y ya vio al doctor." I can hear Mami talking to Mina from our bedroom while my hands press down on my stomach.

"Ahorita, sí, estamos listas." Then the phone slams down, ending the call.

She comes back into my room and sits down on the bed as I

close my eyes and protect myself from the flashing light attacking my window. Under the quilted bedcover with the loose threads and signs of wear, I curl up into a tiny ball, covering my ears from the crashing noises coming from outside.

"Vamos a ir con Mina." I take off the covers and look at Mami.

"Why? I don't feel like going anywhere. Please, Mami, I don't want to go. I just can't right now. Can't she come here?" She places her arm on my back and helps to lift me up.

"She's the expert, and she needs us to go to her house. Diana, ayúdame. Ven con nosotros."

My sister helps my mom guide me into the back seat of our monster mobile. As I lie down, Diana leans over to me.

"You're going to get the egg."

"I'm not hungry . . ." I say. I'm not in the mood to joke, but it feels good to make her laugh.

When we reach the end of the block, Daniela, Mina's daughter, comes to our car window to talk to Mami and then peers into the back.

"What happened to her?" She looks at me, but I turn away, wanting to throw up.

"Rápido, niñas, va a llover. Vamos al cuarto de jugetes. Ponla en la cama," Mina orders, and they rush me inside.

An old and musty mixture tickles my nose. The house is rather new, but inside, it seems too perfect. The tiny bathroom by the kitchen always has the same dusty decorative towels with a wet-dog aroma.

I have been to this house many times. There are three

bedrooms. One is for the parents, one is for Daniela, and the other room is the extra room where Mina does the "egg thing." When I was little, it was my favorite room—full of board games, old dolls, and Barbies. The board games were the best part of the entire room. Every single game you could think of was stacked on those shelves. There was a table in the middle of the room with a chess game in progress. On the floor were individual cases full of every single Barbie that was available. They even had two Kens. That was where we would always meet.

Today I hate this room. Next to the wall, dozens of stuffed animals cover a small bed. Mina places her arm next to the plush display on the bed and sweeps everything off at once.

"Acuéstala aquí." Mami picks me up and places me on the tiny bed. Diana walks out, looking at me with a smirk, wrinkling her nose.

"Where are you going?" I ask. "Stay here."

"No, thanks," she says. "I don't want them to do the egg thing to me. I'm going to find Daniela."

By now Mina is back in the room, holding something in her hand, and she begins to pray over me in fast Spanish with Mami joining in. In the background, I can hear laughter and the piano keys banging. "Chopsticks," maybe.

"Levanta las pijamas." She tells Mami to lift up my pajama top. I now see what she has in her hand, and she rubs it on my stomach. The ice on my skin makes me shake with chills.

"No, Mami, please tell her to stop." I hate the feel of the clammy shell, but she continues to rub it on my back, head, arms, and all over me while the prayers continue. It's freaking me out.

"Santa Maria, Madre de Dios . . ." she repeats, faster and faster.

"What are you doing? You're scaring me!" I say.

Mami reassures me everything's fine.

"Shhhhh, cálmate. Don't worry."

Mina continues praying and rubbing the egg all over my stomach. I just want it to end.

"Please, God, don't let her do anything bad to me."

She looks right into my eyes then and *POPPPP*, she breaks the white shell, pours out the gooey white and yolk in a glass of water, and sets it under the bed.

She is done.

"Ahora sí. Ya la cure del ojo."

"What, what do you mean? Are you sure?"

"Ay, mijita, tienes que entender como trabaja el mundo."

"How can I know how the world works?"

"Mucha gente tiene mal en el corazón. Se ponen celosos y después uno se enferma. Cuando no se alivía uno, es que alguien te hizo ojo. Te vieron con mal intenciones. A lo mejor no te tocaron tu cabeza. Pero no te preocupes; yo se como aliviarte de eso. Te vas a comenzar a sentir mucho mejor."

Mina explains how some people may have evil in their hearts. If an evil-hearted person is jealous of someone or expresses bad intentions, it can make the person sick. And when the person doesn't get well, it means that evil-hearted person didn't touch them after staring at them. That's ojo.

But still. Why was she rubbing an egg on my stomach? How

was that supposed to help? And why was someone supposed to touch my head?

Mami smiles and gives Mina a thank-you hug and then sits on the bed with me. She smiles and hugs me, kissing me on my forehead, and beads of sweat start rolling down my face and back. I close my eyes. They walk out of the room, but I still hear them talking. Until their words fade . . .

~

I don't realize I've fallen asleep until I wake up later. It all seems like a dream, but suddenly my mom and Mina come back into the room.

"Qué bueno que dormiste tanto." Mina reaches under the bed and takes out the glass with the inside of the egg in it, scrutinizing it.

"How long was I asleep? What happened to me?"

"Ves, se quedo arriba del agua. Ya se fue todo el mal." The raw egg stayed at the top of the glass. Mina picks up the glass and holds it as high as she can.

"Gracias a Dios, te vas a aliviar." She lowers the glass and places it right in front of me.

"Mira, mijita, el huevo te dice todo. Ya te curé de ojo!"

Apparently, the egg has spoken. I am cured of mal de ojo, according to Mina. Tomorrow I will have to go back to school. I will have to face Gracie. I hold on to my stomach and wonder . . . does Gracie believe in ojo?

~

The next morning, I arrive at school wearing my favorite bright red jacket and my signature boots, feeling unbelievably perky, and look for Gracie. For some reason, I feel pulled to her.

I approach a table swarming with "it" girls, and Gracie is nestled in their midst, bent over, holding on to her stomach.

Immediately I know why I'm there.

"Hey, Gracie," I say.

She looks up but doesn't say anything.

"Have you ever heard of ojo?"

Her eyes go wide, and that's all the answer I need.

LA LLORONA ISN'T REAL

BY XAVIER GARZA

THIS RIO GRANDE VALLEY

by **DANIEL GARCÍA ORDAZ**

This unforgiving desert, this island paradise,

This meandering killer, this bringer of abundance,

This rich, riparian forest, whose loam feeds nations,

This turbulent, winding waterway of mud-green ripples,

This land of tacos and toil, this land of fearsome, faithful
warriors,

This lush expanse, flattened by shortsighted, hard-charging
pioneers,

This lot of sacrifice and pains, this zone of sleet and windy hurricanes,

This meeting of waters and crossroads of people, this beaten
embankment,

This trampled land, traversed by soldiers, tenanted by
refugees, blessed by saints,

This stand of brambles, sustainer of Native Americans,
Spaniards, Mexicans, and Texans,

This winding tract of royally apportioned soil, this runway to
the lingering sun,

This fertile delta, singer of siren songs, conjunto, mariachi, and
rock 'n' roll,

This thicket of mesquites, this shelter of ocelots, frogs, and
chachalacas,

This sacred spot, this bringer of pilgrims, this launcher of as-
tronauts,

This palm-lined promenade, this temperate wintertime
destination,

This sun-kissed mouth of the river whose people speak in
tongues,

This thorny chaparral, this destroyer of mild men,

This realm of wild horses, this tamer of dreams,

This magical amalgamation, this Valley.

Acknowledgments

Every day, I sit alone with my cup of coffee and give thanks for all my blessings. This whole anthology was a series of fortunate events for me. From an idea that popped into my head to the encouragement from a cherished friend, and everything just kind of fell into place. I must have been born under a lucky star, because I do not know how one person could be blessed with so many wonderful people sent all at the right time to make a dream come true. I am forever grateful.

Lupita McColl, I cannot thank you enough for this. I owe you more than words can say, and more than I could ever repay. Thank you, hermana.

In the beginning, we were so tight-lipped about this project that I didn't have many people to talk to, so I want to thank those few who kept my secret, who helped me keep my head on straight, who figuratively held my hand, who reassured me, who never let me lose focus, who encouraged me to have faith, who told me to burn the bridge that wasn't meant for me, who listened to me ramble, and who guided me. Heart you.

Celina and Lila: my besties por vida.

Justine, Terri, and Adriana: my girl gang.

My big sister Sandy: my biggest fan always.

Tara Connell: my sister from another mister.

Rosie Brock: thank you for all your priceless advice, friendship, and inspiration.

Lucy and Tina: Thank you for your fierce words from the heart, always. #JaneiteSoulSisters #DayOne

Andrea Cascardi: Thank you for taking a chance on a little ol' librarian from the borderlands of Texas. Thank you for your time and your wisdom.

Liza Kaplan: It has been an honor to work with you on this project. You are brilliant at what you do. Thank you for seeing the potential in my idea and in these stories. It is so amazing to finally give it to the world.

To all the *Living Beyond Borders* contributors: you were handpicked for your priceless contributions to Mexican American literature. You are some of the best and most unique voices out there today. Thank you for believing in this project and trusting me with your words and wisdom for our youth. I am honored. Thank you for making one of my wildest dreams come true. Every single one of you is a blessing to me. Abrazos.

And to my mother: I am who I am today because of you. Thank you, Mama. I love you.

In memory of my cousin Jessica Delia Cavazos, my first best friend. A piece of my heart is in heaven with you forever. I miss you and I love you. March 6, 1976–July 12, 2020.

About the Authors

DAVID BOWLES

David Bowles is a Mexican American author from south Texas, where he teaches at the University of Texas Rio Grande Valley. He has written several award-winning titles, most notably *The Smoking Mirror* and *They Call Me Güero*. His work has also been published in multiple anthologies, plus venues such as *The New York Times*, *School Library Journal*, *Strange Horizons*, *English Journal*, *Rattle*, *Translation Review*, and *Journal of Children's Literature*. In 2017 David was inducted into the Texas Institute of Letters.

DOMINIC CARRILLO

Dominic Carrillo is an award-winning writer, speaker, and teacher. His books include *To Be Frank Diego*; *The Improbable Rise of Paco Jones*; *The Unusual Suspects*, which was an IAN Book of the Year Award Finalist; and *Nia and the Dealer*.

ANGELA CERVANTES

Angela Cervantes is an award-winning author of several contemporary middle grade books, including *Lety Out Loud*, a 2020 Pura Belpré Honor Book; *Gaby, Lost and Found*; *Allie, First at Last*; *Me, Frida, and the Secret of the Peacock Ring*, a Junior Library Guild Selection; and *Coco: The Junior Novel*, which accompanied the 2017 blockbuster Disney/Pixar movie.

e. E. CHARLTON-TRUJILLO

e.E. Charlton-Trujillo is a Mexican American filmmaker, literacy activist, and ALA award–winning author who writes picture books, middle grade, and young adult fiction. They are the cofounder of Never Counted Out, a nonprofit that provides access to books and creative mentorship to at-risk youth. Deemed a "force of nature" by *Kirkus Reviews*, Trujillo speaks with humor and heart at festivals, universities, schools, and juvenile detention centers across America, celebrating diversity, inclusivity, and young people being heard. Follow them on social media @pinatadirector or #YourStoryIsARevolution.

RUBÉN DEGOLLADO

Rubén Degollado's work has appeared in *Bilingual Review/La Revista Bilingüe*, *Beloit Fiction Journal*, *Gulf Coast*, *Hayden's Ferry Review*, *Image*, and *Relief*. His debut YA novel, *Throw*, was published in 2019 and won the 2019 Texas Institute of Letters Jean Flynn Award for Best Young Adult Book. His second novel, *The Family Izquierdo*, is forthcoming from W. W. Norton. "La Princesa Mileidy Dominguez" is dedicated to the past, present, and future quinceañeras of San Benito Veterans Memorial Academy and across the Rio Grande Valley of Texas. A special thank-you to the staff and community of SBVMA for making dreams come true.

CAROLYN DEE FLORES

Carolyn Dee Flores is the author and illustrator of *The Amazing Watercolor Fish*, as well as the illustrator of *A Surprise for Teresita*; *Sing, Froggie, Sing*; and *Daughters of Two Nations*. She has won numerous awards and accolades for her work: she was a finalist for the Tomás Rivera Award, received the *Skipping Stones* Award for Multicultural and International Books, was a National Picture Book Champion, and has appeared twice on the Tejas Star Reading List.

GUADALUPE GARCÍA MCCALL

Guadalupe García McCall is an award-winning author and poet. Her debut novel in verse, *Under the Mesquite*, received the prestigious Pura Belpré Author Award, was a William C. Morris Award Finalist, received the International Literacy Association Lee Bennett Hopkins Promising Poet Award and the Tomás Rivera Children's Book Award, and was included in *Kirkus Reviews'* 2011 Best Books for Teens, among many other accolades. Her second novel, *Summer of the Mariposas*, won a Westchester Young Adult Fiction Award, was a finalist for the Andre Norton Award for Young Adult Science Fiction and Fantasy, and was included in the 2013 Amelia Bloomer Project List, the Texas Lone Star Reading List, and *School Library Journal's* 2012 Best Books of the Year. Her poems for children have appeared in *The Poetry Friday Anthology, I Remember: Poems and Pictures of Heritage*, and *No Voice Too Small: Fourteen Young Americans Making History*. Her third novel, *Shame the Stars*, received a *Kirkus* starred review, was listed on the TAYSHAS Reading List, and was chosen as the 2018 Texas Great Read by the Center for the Book, Her most recently published book, *All the Stars Denied*, was a 2018 Writers' League of Texas Book Award Finalist as well as a 2019 Texas Institute of Letters YA Book Award Finalist. She has a fifth book, her first gothic novel, *Echoes of Grace*, forthcoming from Tu Books in 2022.

DANIEL GARCÍA ORDAZ

Daniel García Ordaz, also known as the Poet Mariachi, is the author of *Cenzontle/Mockingbird: Songs of Empowerment* and *You Know What I'm Sayin'?* García Ordaz, an educator and songwriter, is also a founder of the Rio Grande Valley International Poetry Festival and an established voice in Mexican American poetry.

XAVIER GARZA

Xavier Garza is an award-winning author of *Creepy Creatures and Other Cucuys; Lucha Libre: The Man in the Silver Mask: A Bilingual Cuento; Juan and the Chupacabras/Juan y el Chupacabras; Charro Claus and the Texas Kid; Zulema and the Witch Owl/Zulema y la Bruja Lechuza; Kid Cyclone Fights the Devil and Other Stories/Kid Ciclon Se Enfrenta a el Diablo y Otras Historias; Maximilian & the Mystery of the Guardian Angel: A Bilingual Lucha Libre Thriller; Maximilian & the Bingo Rematch: A Lucha Libre Sequel; The Great and Mighty Nikko; The Donkey Lady Fights la Llorona and Other Stories;* and *Maximilian & the Lucha Libre Club: A Bilingual Lucha Libre Thriller.* He has been honored with the Pure Belpré Honor, and his books are on several reading lists including Tejas Star and Texas Institute of Letters.

TRINIDAD GONZALES

Trinidad Gonzales is a history instructor at South Texas College and a cofounder of Refusing to Forget, an award-winning nonprofit public-history project devoted to bringing awareness to state-sanctioned violence against ethnic Mexicans that occurred during the 1910s in Texas. Gonzales has published op-ed pieces in *Austin American-Statesmen, San*

Antonio Express-News, and *The Monitor* concerning issues of immigra-
tion and Mexican American studies. His scholarly publications deal
with issues of identity, borderlands, and Mexican American politics.
He also taught the first dual-enrollment Mexican American studies
course in Texas at Mission High School. Gonzales is a former American
Historical Association Teaching Division councilor and continues to
advise on the AHA Texas Conference on Introductory History Courses
that he helped begin.

DIANA LÓPEZ
Diana López is the author of *Sofia's Saints* and numerous middle grade
novels, including *Confetti Girl*; *Nothing Up My Sleeve*; *Lucky Luna*; and
Coco: A Story about Music, Shoes, and Family, a middle grade adaption of
the Disney/Pixar film *Coco*.

ANNA MERIANO
Anna Meriano is the author of the Love Sugar Magic series and *This Is
How We Fly*. She graduated from Rice University with a degree in English
and earned her MFA in creative writing with an emphasis in writing for
children from the New School in New York. She works as a writing teacher
and tutor in her hometown of Houston. Anna likes reading, knitting, and
playing full-contact quidditch.

JUSTINE MARIE NARRO
Justine Marie Narro is a poet from the Rio Grande Valley. She holds a BA
in English literature. Her poems have been published on various websites,
and she is an open-mic poet around the Rio Grande Valley.

GUADALUPE RUIZ-FLORES
Guadalupe Ruiz-Flores is the author of six award-winning bilingual chil-
dren's picture books published by Arte Público Press: *Let's Salsa*, *Lupita's
First Dance*, *Alicia's Fruity Drinks*, *The Battle of the Snow Cones*, *The
Woodcutter's Gift*, and *Lupita's Papalote*. Her books have appeared on the
Tejas Star Reading List on numerous occasions. Some of her poetry has
been published in anthologies.

AIDA SALAZAR

Aida Salazar is the award-winning author of the verse novel *The Moon Within* (International Latino Book Award, Américas Award Honor, Golden Poppy Award) and the critically acclaimed *Land of the Cranes*. She also authored the picture books *Jovita Wore Pants: The Story of a Revolutionary Fighter* and *In the Spirit of a Dream: 13 Stories of Immigrants of Color*. Her work has received starred reviews from *Kirkus Reviews*, *School Library Journal*, and *Publishers Weekly*. She is a founding member of Las Musas, a Latinx kidlit author collective. Her story "By the Light of the Moon" was adapted into a ballet by the Sonoma Conservatory of Dance and is the first Xicana-themed ballet in history.

RENÉ SALDAÑA JR.

René Saldaña Jr. is an associate professor of language, diversity, and literacy studies in the College of Education at Texas Tech University. He is also the author of many young adult and middle grade novels, which include *The Jumping Tree*, *The Whole Sky Full of Stars*, *A Good Long Way*, and the bilingual flip-book Mickey Rangel detective mystery series. He is the editor of a YA poetry anthology on body image titled *I SING: THE BODY*.

SYLVIA SÁNCHEZ GARZA

Sylvia Sánchez Garza grew up in Weslaco, Texas, and now lives in Edinburg, Texas, with her husband, sons, and dogs. She enjoys spending time with her family and friends and serving the culturally rich and beautiful community of the Rio Grande Valley. As a former teacher and a current school board member, Sylvia values education and is grateful for the opportunities that have been given to her. She holds a BA in English, an MA in school administration, and a PhD in leadership studies. *Cascarones*, a coming-of-age novel about the cultures and traditions of growing up as a Mexican American in South Texas, was her first book, published by Floricanto Press. It has won several awards, including a Literary Classics Gold Star, a Texas Writer Award, and a Literary Titan Silver Book Award. Garza is presently working on a YA novel as well as a poetry manuscript.

FRANCISCO X. STORK

Francisco X. Stork emigrated from Mexico at the age of nine with his mother and stepfather. He is the author of eight novels, including *Marcelo in the Real World*, recipient of the Schneider Family Book Award; *The Last Summer of the Death Warriors*, which received the Elizabeth Walden Award; *The Memory of Light*, recipient of the Tomás Rivera Award; and *Disappeared*, which received four starred reviews and was a Walter Dean Myers Award Honor Book.

ALEX TEMBLADOR

Alex Temblador is the Mixed Latinx author of the YA novel *Secrets of the Casa Rosada*, which received a starred review from *Kirkus Reviews*, won the 2019 NACCS Tejas Foco Young Adult Fiction Award, was a *Kirkus Reviews* Best Young Adult Book of 2018, won the 2018 Middle Grade/Young Adult Discovery Prize from the Writers' League of Texas, and was included on Texas Library Association's 2020 TAYSHAS Reading List. In addition to her upcoming adult magical realism novel, *Half Outlaw*, Alex's creative work has appeared in *PALABRITAS* and *Speculative Fiction for Dreamers: A Latinx Anthology*. The Dallas-based author is a creative writing instructor and moderator of Dallas–Fort Worth's author panel series LitTalk, as well as a public speaker on diversity, equity, and inclusion initiatives, and a freelance travel, arts, and design writer for internationally known publications.